HERE IS WHAT YOU DO

HERE IS WHAT YOU DO

Stories

CHRIS DENNIS

SOHO

Published by Soho Press
853 Broadway
New York, NY 10003

Library of Congress Cataloging-in-Publication Data

Dennis, Chris, 1979–
Here is what you do : stories / Chris Dennis.
Description: New York, NY : Soho Press, 2019.
I. Title.

ISBN 978-1-64129-036-4
eISBN 978-1-64129-037-1

PS3604.E58634 A6 2019 813'.6—dc23 2019001350

Interior design by Janine Agro, Soho Press, Inc.

Printed in the United States of America

10 9 8 7 6 5 4 3 2 1

For Zaden, my everything.

"It's all wrong but it's all right."

—DOLLY PARTON

HERE IS WHAT YOU DO

Contents

Here Is What You Do

You wet your hair in the sink, then comb it back, slick as a new trash bag. You look nice. Okay, so your name is Ricky. You are twenty-three years old. People say you're sweet. You say to them, "No, I'm not." But you are. You know you are. You can't help it. It's like there's a piece of candy hidden deep inside you and everyone is trying to find the easiest way to get it out.

Your cellmate, Donald Budke, he's like Rasputin, or Genghis Khan, maybe even Napoleon Bonaparte. No one tells Donald he's sweet. His motives are serious, and he's got acne scars that make him look like a criminal. He is a criminal. He's ten years older than you, is on his fourth year of a fifteen-year sentence for manslaughter. You're just a high school history teacher from southern Indiana, or at least you used to be.

On the day you were arrested, the US Customs agent said, "What the hell are you doing, Ricky?" like he knew you or something, like he was really disappointed. "Who's the vehicle registered to, Ricky?" You told him it was your grandmother's.

You gave him your driver's license, your car keys. He asked you to sit in the back of his patrol car while he searched your trunk. You watched through the windshield, waiting for him to find the five cottage-cheese containers full of oxycodone you'd hidden beneath the spare tire. The sky was pink, like a drop of blood in a glass of water. You thought, Mexico is like an art film. You thought about the ten or so pills in the pocket of your pants, wished there was some way of keeping them so you could eat them later, in the event you were placed under arrest. You didn't want to eat any of them right then. You were already as high as a butterfly. You fished the handful out of your jeans pocket and put two in your mouth anyway, waited for the spit to come, swallowed. The rest you chewed into a paste and spat onto the floorboard of the patrol car while the Customs agent rifled through your roadside emergency kit.

The man came back and said, "You need to step out of the car, Ricky."

Before the Customs agent put you back in the car, he said, "Anything else hidden on your person becomes a felony inside the jail. Is there anything else, Ricky?" You stared at his ears, which were so big and red. They suited him, you thought.

"No, sir," you said. "Where else would I put it?"

"Never mind," he said, looking away.

You could hardly hold your eyes open.

Hours later inside the Customs office, another man—not much older than you, his eyes pale as pool water—told you to relax your hand while he rolled your fingers across an ink pad, pressing the fingertips onto a little index card with your name on it. The fingerprinting station was fascinating, and you told him so. You talked to him about Henry Faulds, a squat man, you said, who wore funny hats, credited with being the first person to use fingerprints for identification. "He used a greasy print left on a bottle of alcohol," you said.

"Well, all right then," the man said.

He put you in a small room by yourself, a concrete cell with pale green walls and no windows. You lay down on a metal bench that was bolted to the floor. You drifted in and out of the thing the pills made you feel. You thought about Horatio Nelson and the final moments in the battle of Cape St. Vincent—the fleets falling out of formation on the water, gun smoke rising toward the sails, Nelson reaching out to take the surrendering sword of *San José*. You slept, turning constantly on the hard bench, shaking the whole time from nervousness and the thought of never going home and the thought of not having any more pills to take. The lights went off, and then later came back on again. A man opened the door to say you could use the phone. You followed him into the racket of the booking office and called your nanny.

"Good afternoon," Nanny said when she answered the phone. You tried to explain about the pills but she kept saying, "Ricky, how did this happen? Should I come get you?" When you said you were in Texas she started to cry. That wasn't the worst part.

"Who's done this to you? Should I call the police?" she asked. There was a loud crash on the other end of the phone, something breaking.

"What was that, Nanny?"

"I dropped a plate of food. Where's the car, Ricky?"

"I'm being arrested, Nanny. I have the car. I'll bring it back."
And you meant it, without even realizing you wouldn't be able
to. She said she'd call the secretary at Woodrow Wilson High
School to tell them you wouldn't be at work on Monday. She
told you not to worry about the dogs, she'd find someone else to
walk them. This made you feel deserted, and damned. Nanny
didn't get it. "Can the neighbors do it?" you asked. Nanny said
she had to go, to clean up the food.

"Nanny! Nanny!" you said after she hung up.

THE OFFICER NEXT to you reached for his Taser. You
dropped to the floor and hid your face. "Jesus," he said, before
helping you up.

After two weeks in the Webb County Jail, Judge Henry Trav-
ers of the eleventh circuit court sentenced you to one year at
Lewis Unit in Woodville, Texas. "You'll only serve four months,"
your public defender said afterward.

You spent eight days in a holding cell with a car thief named
Teddy from Houston, then walked down a long, loud hall full of
men yelling and watching as the guard took you to your room.
Donald was sitting on the edge of the bunk, reading. The guard
handed you your toiletries. The door made a shocking click-
clicking noise when it closed. Donald moved his hair out of his
eyes, held out his hand for you to shake.

"You like Tom Clancy?" Donald asked, showing you the
cover of his book.

Most of the cells here are two-man rooms with bunk beds, like the one you're in. There are three dormitories with around seventy men in each and people get moved all of the time but you've been in the two-man cell with Donald since your intake. Everywhere you turn there are black men. They huddle in the dorms, or else move through the block like schools of shimmering fish spotted by the rare scrawl of a white face. When the white men smile, their slim mouths are filled with rotten teeth. At first there is a lot of crying and vomiting and shaking, coming off the beautiful pain pills you'd grown, over the past year and a half, to love enormously. This is prison. Donald says he can't find you pills in here and that anyone who can is looking for a hookup. Sometimes the old dudes will offer something boring at the canteen, Effexor or Ambien. These do not help.

You look at yourself a lot in the mirror. You're lanky—bony and gaunt. Your hair is too blond, the cut pathetically neat. Everyone in here seems taller than you. Even the shortest felon seems like a giant.

Donald tells you that some of the other inmates have offered him money for the chance to get at you. "What do you mean?" you ask.

"What do you call a blond with half a brain?" he asks.

Two months in and already you are ashamed of so many things, things you had no idea a person could be ashamed of. One, for being educated, because most of the men here never made it through high school. You feel embarrassed around them, like Louis XVI must have felt after his arrest, surrounded by the working class in the Temple prison—not condescending but humiliated.

Your cell has a toilet with a sink attached. The sink is attached to the top of the toilet where you think the tank should be. At first this made you uncomfortable about washing your hands. You're used to it now. You have to straddle the toilet facing the tank or stand to the side of it when you brush your teeth, or wash, or get a drink. You push a button above the faucet and the water comes.

The recreation room reminds you of the teachers' lounge at Woodrow Wilson High. One of the dudes in there, he can hardly read the newspaper. When you first saw him, sitting with the paper open, sounding out the words to himself, you thought you'd help him. He was skipping the words he couldn't figure out. You went over and pulled up a chair. "Can I have a look?" you said. This was before you knew how things worked.

He said, "Get your own fucking paper."

"It's *nay*-borhood," you told him, "not *neeg*-borhood."

"I got it," he said, sliding his chair away. "Now get the fuck off me you faggoty fuck."

"Sorry," you said.

Your lip was trembling. You couldn't think of anything good to say. You got up and went to the other side of the room. You sat in one of the yellow vinyl lounge chairs next to the window, pretending to read *People* magazine. You sit there a lot now. You try not to make eye contact with anyone you suspect might be illiterate.

You told Donald the story and he laughed. You pretended to

laugh too, but also you were crying a little. You didn't let Donald know.

Donald has long, black hair. Many tattoos. His teeth aren't perfect, but you've seen worse. There is something dim and monumental in his eyes—the irises gray as tombstones. He grew up in Iowa. You can hear it when he talks. He calls cola "pop," and other things like that. This is not the only reason you like Donald but it has a lot to do with it. He says he's in for manslaughter, but he won't say anything else. You ask him what happened but instead he talks about his hair. "There were a few guys in here that used to fuck with me," he says, "because I wouldn't cut my hair and because sometimes I put it up in a ponytail. They used to say to me, 'What's under the ponytail, Donald, a horse's ass?' All I have to do now is give them the look."

He stands up really fast, like something bad has just happened. You're not sure what's going on. He gets right up in front of you like he's considering the quickest way to crack open your face. "That's what I do," he says. "That's the look I give them." He starts laughing. "Works, don't it?"

You nod. Your pulse knocks inside your ears. "It does. For real."

He says now he tells them to shut the fuck up and they shut the fuck up. You're sure you're not capable of this.

"Try it," he says.

"I don't think so. I'll just be cool. I'll stay out of their way or else give them my dessert at dinner."

Donald points his finger at you. "Shut the fuck up!" he yells.

He makes a fist, brings it up to your mouth and presses the knuckles against your lips. "Stop fucking talking right now!"

"Why? What did I do wrong?" you say into his knuckles.

"No, Ricky. Damn it. That's what you're supposed to say to them. I'm not telling you to shut the fuck up. Shit, dude, you've got to stop being such a giant pussy." Donald shakes his head, like he can't believe people like you exist. "I'm trying to help you," he says. "You're going to be in here a really long time. You've got to at least try."

You've been here two months now. "Yeah," you say, "two more months."

"You'll be lucky if they ever let you out," Donald says. He picks up his book. *Without Remorse*, it's called, and it must be serious because Donald will sometimes talk aloud while he's reading, usually to cuss out the bad guys who he says are always corrupt cops. He lies down on the bed holding the book open in front of his face. "It's gonna suck without you here, man."

You've been with him almost every hour of every day since you got here and you're still not sure what to do when he says these things.

He lays the book down on his chest. He says, "Some dudes make friends in here and then get all depressed if they leave. You're lucky I'm not like that. I'd never try to kill myself or anything." He picks up the book again. "I'm reading now, don't talk to me." He stares at it, turns a page. "Bitch," he says, and then, "Just kidding."

Another thing you feel ashamed for is Donald. You can't remember ever thinking of a man in this way. You had a girlfriend for a while in college, Janice Pickett. You looked at her and you liked what you saw. She was short, breasts like half-filled water balloons, strawberry-blond hair. On the old couch in your dorm room, spring of sophomore year, she took your virginity. She took off your clothes and sat on your lap. There was a sudden wetness on you, like maybe she'd just spilled warm soup on your penis. You made an awkward groan and came inside her. She got up and ran to the bathroom. After that you went on dates together to the movies and to sports bars. You bought flavored condoms and laid a blanket down on the dorm-room floor, thought about important moments of the American Civil War and tried not to come as soon as she climbed on top of you. You liked her, thought about asking if she wanted to move in together. Right before graduation she showed up saying, "Let's keep in touch, Ricky. Sound good?" But it sounded awful, like she was making fun of you or something. That was two years ago. You haven't had a woman since. The female teachers at Woodrow Wilson made you nervous when they started acting sexy, cornering you in front of the faculty microwave. You just never thought about guys. One time in college a drunk guy at a house party showed his penis to everyone in the room. It made your face hot, caused a tingling feeling in your stomach, but you didn't want to touch it or anything. Why would you? You only thought it looked weird. It was big.

When you find out that Nanny reported the car stolen, her car, which you drove from Indiana to Mexico to buy the pills, you aren't angry exactly, just frustrated. Frustrated is a better word for it. Nanny forgets things. She can't help it.

She can't come to visit but you call her on Thursdays. At first she only asked about the car, kept telling you that someone had stolen it. "Can you believe someone would do that to me?" she said. Two months in and she's finally stopped with that. Instead she tells you she hopes you're doing well, that she's proud of you, and proud of your new job in Pittsburgh, where she says you're teaching history again. She says you should go and straighten up the desks before class every day, pick up all the little bits of paper trash off the floor so that the Lord can come into a nice clean classroom before each session, inspiring the children to learn and truly love their lessons. "Will you do that for me, Ricky? Will you try it and see if it makes a difference?"

"Yes," you say, "I'll do that, for sure, what a good idea." Then you walk back down the hall, through all the loud and mechanical doors toward your cell, where Donald is playing rummy against himself or watching *The Maury Povich Show*.

"How was it?" he says.

"Oh, it was whack," you tell him.

At nine o'clock the lights and the television are shut off. Sometimes it takes a while for the cell block to quiet down. The other inmates are always laughing or yelling. Eventually one of the guards calls for everyone to knock it off. Donald has the bottom bunk, and he usually waits fifteen or so minutes before he asks if you're asleep. You say, "No, I'm still awake," and then Donald asks if you want to come down there.

"Whatever," you say.

You'd been in here maybe a month when Donald first said it, and now after a few weeks of it, you just climb down from your bunk and try not to look nervous. You wait for him to make a spot for you next to the wall. You lie stiff as a book against the cold concrete and wait. You both lie there for a minute without touching until he asks if you want to suck. That's when the tingling in your stomach starts. If you want to suck you put your hand on his penis, which is already so hard that it sticks up out of his underwear, flat against his stomach under the tight elastic of his briefs. You play with it for a minute before putting your face under the covers. Sometimes he asks if you'd rather fuck, in which case you roll over and face the wall. It's nothing, really. Just a heavy weight. A heat in your joints. A current traveling. This is what cellmates do.

About the pills. You had an abscessed tooth, right—a cavity and then a pain like a wide throb across your face that woke you up one morning before work. Your dentist—the same one Nanny had been taking you to since you were little—scolded you for letting it get that bad, prescribed ten days' worth of antibiotics and twenty Vicodin, told you to come back in a week and a half. The first pain pill made you dizzy and tired. You slept straight through the night. The second one made you vomit. The third one lit a glorious fire in your head that eventually spread to your chest and arms and groin until it had invaded your whole body. Everything was right in the world. Nanny was a thin, white angel mixing vanilla pudding at the kitchen table. The children at school were blurs of pink and green with flesh tones in between. Instead of reading aloud from the textbook every day you wrote lectures for the first time. History books became the things they used to be on sunnier days alone in your old dorm room. The surge of those sagas opened up to you like ancient mausoleums.

You read:

"The Life of Wilhelm Conrad Roentgen."
The Sephardim in the Ottoman Empire.
A History of the American Privateers, and Letters-of-Marque During Our War with England in the Years 1812, '13 and '14.

You could put your hand over your eyes and see battlefields, crowded infirmaries, the torchlit corridors of Nubian pyramids.

After that you were making appointments at the doctor's office all the time, complaining of back pain, neck pain, chronic headaches, a burning sensation in your kneecaps. You'd take Lortab, Vicodin, Percocet, Percodan, Tylox. It was like learning a secret language. Some of the pills were more exciting than others. You saw three different doctors, had prescriptions filled at every drugstore in town, until finally Shirley Lynn Dobbs at Dobbs' Drugstore started asking questions, making calls.

It was maybe a week later that you saw the article about pharmaceuticals and drug laws in *Newsweek*—they mentioned Mexico, speedy clinics in the backs of grocery stores and novelty shops, prescriptions for anything a patient was willing to pay for in cash. You thought of nineteenth-century China, of the thriving opium trade and those covert smoking divans. It sounded like the most perfect retreat.

It was the Thanksgiving holiday. You told Nanny you were

going to Indianapolis to hear a seminar on the Miami Indians of the Midwest. You emptied your savings, cashed in a couple of bonds. You had enough pills to last three days. You got in Nanny's car and drove. And drove. And drove. The sun and the moon came and went.

The day before Thanksgiving, in Nuevo Laredo, you rented a room at the Red Roof Inn. You got lost two days in a row, ate too many cheap enchiladas, asked the wrong people the wrong questions in the wrong language until you finally decided that the back-door pharmacies were made up, were more like small invisible cities of El Dorado than the luxurious opium dens of China.

On the last night, at the Chaser Lounge, you let Kenny Voglar from Carson City, Nevada, buy you too many strawberry margaritas. Kenny wore a lime-green tank top and a diamond ring. He claimed he was once the president of the Rod Stewart fan club. He had a soft spot for GHB and Xanax. He said he knew a man who had exactly what you were looking for. You could see your reflection in the mirror behind the bar. The Christmas lights strung around the alcohol bottles made little flashes of color across your face like so many blue and red stars blinking off and on.

The man who had exactly what you were looking for was actually a seventeen-year-old Mexican kid in short-shorts with a Madonna tattoo. Kenny talked. The Mexican kid turned up "Like a Prayer" on the stereo and danced. Kenny watched. You stood by the door, pretending to read the ingredients on a package of gum. After the song was over the kid went into the bathroom, made some noise, brought out five cottage-cheese containers full of pills. He handed you one of the pills. You took it, and sat on the floor watching the Hispanic boy and Kenny Voglar snort something off the bedside table. They danced around to the music while you waited for the pill to do its stuff. After twenty minutes or so you decided you maybe liked Madonna. "Vogue" seemed like an interesting song. The Hispanic kid did a special dance for it. He seemed very talented. You gave him all of your money. He gave you all of his cottage-cheese containers.

If you don't answer Donald when he asks if you're asleep, he says, "I see how it is. What? You mad at me? You got a problem, Ricky?" But you're never mad at him. You're just worried. You lie in your bed and fake the loud, steady breaths of deep sleep. You feel the bed start to shake, Donald furiously taking care of himself on the bunk beneath. He's only touched your penis once, wrapped his hand around it and squeezed for a second. After he finishes in your mouth or on your back he quickly pulls up his pants and rolls over and you climb up to your bunk.

Once, after he was finished fucking, you started to get up and he said, "Don't move." He put his arms around you, pressed his face into your back, touched you neatly on the spine with his nose. You might have stayed like that all night except Donald woke you up later, smacking you in the head, saying, "Go back to your own bed, faggot." An inmate a couple of cells down was yelling, "It's my stomach. I think it's the pancreas! I need a doctor!"

"Shut the hell up," someone else yelled.

"No shit," Donald called back, "because you don't even know what a pancreas is!"

You met with your drug counselor for the first time and he told you your official release date. May 14. It is now the fifth of April. He said he was proud of you, which was odd since you'd only met with him once. Still, it was nice to hear. You asked when you would have to appear before the parole board. He said, "This is a kind of parole hearing right now. You've done everything right. Good job, Ricky."

You come back into the cell and tell Donald that things went great with the counselor. Donald is sitting on the floor, shuffling the cards. "Where's *Rainbow Six*?"

"Where's what?"

"My new Clancy book, idiot. Where the fuck is it?"

"I haven't seen it."

Donald holds up the deck of cards with one hand, presses them between his thumb and index finger so that the cards go flying. There's something in his mouth. He looks up at you while the cards fly. He spits hard across the room, hitting you, perfectly, on the mouth. He says, "Don't think you're better than anyone else in here! You fucking drug addict. If you get out you'll be back on drugs in no time. Then you'll be dead."

You stand with his spit running down your chin. You want to say something but the spit clings. You don't wipe it away. Just stare at the wall with your mouth closed tight. You think about the Korean War. Think about President Harry S. Truman or picture old Douglas MacArthur standing on the grassy banks of the Nakdong River, polishing his sunglasses with a handkerchief.

Wait for Donald to look away and then use your shirtsleeve to wipe away the spit. You go and put your mouth under the spigot. You wonder how much tobacco it must have taken General MacArthur to fill his gigantic pipe. Think about your counselor. Think: Good job, Ricky. Good job.

Nanny is your mother, or she might as well be. There has never been anyone else, at least not that you can remember. You remember a day years ago, before the pills, right after you moved home from college. You were in the living room with Nanny. The dogs, Ashley and Lyle, were asleep under the coffee table, their noses at Nanny's feet. She sat her Dr Pepper down on the china saucer she used for a coaster. You loved the sound it made after each drink, when she returned the can to the saucer, the warbled ping of aluminum to china. "You know, honey, to me Dr Pepper tastes like vanilla extract. And you know what else? I think you have always been this way. You have always been like you are now, even as a little boy. A criminal mind, some people call it, but I think you could be a minister. Your great-grandfather was insane. He used to choke rabbits to death in the shed. He enjoyed it. You remind me of him." You were flattered, even though it was clearly one of her less coherent days and you weren't entirely sure what she meant. She kept calling you Larry, who was maybe an old friend of hers. She'd go through a short list of names—her grandfather, distant cousins—before she called you by the right one. It made you proud to know you reminded her of a dangerous person. You only wished you were the sort of person who could choke a bunny. You wonder if Nanny somehow knew this was coming.

The day after Donald spat in your face the two of you sit on the floor and play spades as if none of it happened. Donald has a tattoo of a black knife surrounded by a spiral of thorns directly over his Adam's apple. You stare at his throat, not at the tattoo, but at the thick apex of bone there. It reminds you of something. A pill. A tree. An erection.

"One time I choked a rabbit to death," you tell him.

"My lawyer fucked me over, really did a number on me," he says.

"What do you mean?"

"Just did, man. Just did."

This isn't good enough. You want the history. The timeline of events. You want the body count. But before you can ask him, Donald reaches into his pants and takes out an oatmeal cookie. "I saved it from lunch. It's all yours." It's against the rules to leave the mainline with food, and you don't like oatmeal cookies. But you eat it anyway. Donald says, "Ricky, I was trying to help you. That's why I spit on you. Every motherfucker in here is going to try and spit in your face, or worse. They don't give a shit whether you live or die. You're not free yet, man. You're still an inmate. I just want you to be prepared. I just really care about you. I take care of me and mine."

During the last few weeks you keep your hands clean. Shave every day. When you shower, you always use more soap on the parts of you Donald pays most attention to: hands, butt, hands.

Nanny sends many cards. The last one: *Life is well in Pike County. Ashley is eight! Lyle has been injured! Those crazy people down the street with the camouflage golf cart! Ashley whines at your bedroom door. Lyle always thought so much of you. You didn't forget about him, did you? He would always follow you around when you killed the flies so he could eat up the dead ones! Went to lunch at Long John Silver's with my sister. She's been coming over to walk the dogs. I might get tired of her soon! Been thinking of you. Been thinking of you so much. Submitted your name to the prayer chain at church.*

Climb into bed. Get back up. Read the last chapter in all of Donald's books. Write a letter to Nanny. Drink water from the sink. Wet your hair. Comb it straight back. Look at yourself in the metal of the sink and think: *Not bad, Ricky.*

You like the black guys but sometimes they throw pieces of food at each other during dinner. They make a mess. They ask you what you're looking at and you offer them your fruit cup. One of them comes and takes it. "Thank you," he says. Apparently he doesn't like the pear chunks, because he spends the rest of the time throwing them back at you every time the guard looks away. Finally Donald comes in and sits down, sees the pear chunks on the table, a piece stuck to the front of your jumpsuit. He looks over at the black dudes but they're looking at their food, pushing it around with their spoons. "What the fuck?" Donald says. Eventually someone lifts his head. Donald points at him, picks up some of the pear, throws it and hits him right on the forehead. They both stand up.

"Fuck no," Donald says. "Sit right back down." When the guy doesn't sit down, you say to Donald, "Don't. Just forget about it. I don't care about the pears," but Donald is walking over with his tray in his hands and breaking it over the guy's head. One swift crack against the man's face and the guards are dragging Donald out of the mainline. You're just standing there, not saying a word, with fruit still stuck on your jumpsuit.

Donald's skin is tan and tough from years of working in the sun. He was a laborer. He roofed hotels in Cleveland, worked as a garbage man in Louisville, did other things in Chicago, "You go where the work is," he always says.

He is gone for over a week. In solitary confinement. You can only wonder what is happening to him. Sometimes men will spend months in the hole. No television. No books. No one to talk to. Donald came on you the night before he hit the guy in the face with the food tray. You don't take a bath while he's gone. You keep the smell on you. Put your hands on your back, between your legs, up to your nose. It is the smell of something old, something unclean and sour and terribly personal. This is what it's like with him.

Several inmates approach you in the yard. They enclose you, dark and scary as a basement. They want to know if you're looking for anything. One of them gets right up in your face. He says, "You're fair game now that your dude is gone."

He tells you, "This way, buddy. Walk over here." But one of the senior guards, Clint maybe, or Gary, comes and stands between the two of you.

He says, "Come on, Ricky. That's enough. Let's go." He takes you through the gymnasium, and all the way back to your cell. "You need to get your shit together," he says. He wants to know how a kid like you ended up in Woodville.

"Drugs," you tell him.

He laughs at that. "What else," he says. It's not a question.

You lie in bed the rest of the time smelling yourself and thinking about Donald: how he only sleeps on his back; how the blood pools in the sink after he brushes his teeth; how he always cleans under his fingernails with an envelope, how his semen tastes, how it sprays over you in varying arcs—the distance it goes, the sheer and warm amount of it shooting across your body.

When he finally comes back you're in the recreation room sitting in your chair by the window, reading a magazine. You watch him walk in. He's freshly shaven. His hair is pulled back, combed and wet. You're not sure if you should smile. You know you pay too much attention to him in front of other people. He stands on the other side of the room talking to some of the other men from your block. He looks so clean, just back from the showers. You're still dirty. You walk over and stand next to him. You don't speak. It takes him a minute. "What's up?" he says, like he hardly knows you. You have to keep your hands tucked into your waistband to keep from reaching out and stroking his ponytail. Here you are, like Hephaestion standing in the court of Alexander the Great, pretending to listen to the strategies but instead thinking of how he's going to make you feel after the troops disperse.

When you're both back in the cell Donald says, "They'll put someone else in here as soon as you're gone. I wonder who it will be? I hope they're cool."

You imagine another man in the cell. You imagine the lights going out, the room quiet for a few minutes before Donald asks this other man if he's asleep. You wonder what Donald means by "cool."

At lights-out you take all of your clothes off and wait for him to ask you. After maybe half an hour has passed and he hasn't said anything you climb down and get into his bed. For the first time, you kiss him. Maybe you shouldn't but you want to try.

"What the hell?" he says, jerking back, like he doesn't understand. "I'm not your fucking boyfriend." He grabs your head, pushes you down toward his crotch. "Do me a favor," he says.

For the rest of the week, after lights-out, Donald says nothing or else he just comes up to your bunk. He says, "Turn over." He presses his fist against the small of your back and whispers in your ear. He says, "You like it now, don't you? You love it. You want me to own it." He says, "You like it when it hurts?"

You tell him you like it when it hurts. You tell him you want him to own you.

You talk to Nanny on the phone. You tell her you need a way to get back to Indiana. You tell her the car was impounded, you don't have the car, she'll have to pick it up.

Nanny is upset. "Ricky, you've got a good job there in Pittsburgh. It's a friendly city. I don't know why you're quitting. This is nonsense." So many times you've explained to Nanny. It was easier to go along at first, but now you realize the problem with that.

You tell her it's the end of the school year and you might go back in the fall but you're not sure yet. You say there's been some conflict among the faculty members over trash in the classrooms. "I don't know what to do," you say. You ask for money to buy a plane ticket. You tell her she can send it to the same address she sends the letters. She says she has to get the dog off her lap. "I have an ink pen right here," she says. You've given her the address four other times, but you tell her again. She says, "Why on earth would I mail a check to someplace in Texas, Ricky? That doesn't make any sense to me." You get the dreadful feeling that maybe she chooses her moments of sanity. Nanny says that Ashley is going crazy over something in the kitchen, probably a mouse behind the refrigerator. She has to get off the phone to see what the ruckus is about. "I can't have her hurting herself. They're all I've got, Ricky. These sweet little dogs." She hangs up and for a while you keep the receiver to your ear, listening to the droning static of the open line until the guard taps on the door to say your time is up.

After dinner you and Donald play cards and drink milk, sharing the same Styrofoam cup, taking little sips so that there is always another drink left. You always do it this way when you have milk before bed, and there is always one last sip. Even before the lights are turned off you put your hands down the front of Donald's underwear. You hold his penis. Donald punches you in the arm and then puts his hand in your underwear too. He tries jacking you off. You each hold the other's penis. Donald doesn't know what he's doing. He gets too rough. You think he's trying to make it hurt. You don't say it hurts though and, eventually, it starts to feel good.

The lights go out before you're done.

"Stay here," he says.

"Where?"

"Here, idiot. With me."

"I don't think I can."

"Then do something," he says, smiling.

"What do you mean?"

"I already said."

You get in Donald's bed. He puts his head under the cover. Puts you in his mouth. He bites you. You're wishing you knew how to help him. You're wishing he knew what he was doing, that he meant it. His teeth get in the way. He's going too fast.

"Are you close?" he says.

"I think so," you say.

He moves around for a few minutes. He presses his thumbs into your thighs. Eventually he gives up, slides back onto the pillow and props his head on an arm. He uses his other hand on you. He stares at you while he does it. He's never let you be this close to his face but after a minute he is finally putting his lips close to yours, easing his tongue in your mouth. He opens too wide and breathes across your teeth until you are running out over his knuckles and down onto your stomach. He's right there in front of you and you can feel his mouth widening into a smile. Something shifts, spreads through your body like a vivid fluid crowding out your limbs.

"You don't want to leave," he says. "I've got fifteen more years of this fucking place. Think about that."

"Eleven," you say. "You've got eleven more years."

"Yeah," he says. "Eleven. That's what I meant."

"Why?"

"I ran over a dog."

"Did the dog belong to someone famous?"

"No. Moron." He's quiet. He sits up, then lies down again. "Do you have kids?" he says.

"You know I don't." It's like he's forgotten who he's even talking to.

"That's right, you don't. They're not what you expect. It's not like how you imagine. You think you can look at someone else's kids and know what it's like." Donald lets down his ponytail. The hair falls forward, hiding his face. "When they're yours it's like they're wild animals or something and you have to clean up their shit and keep them from burning the house down or running into the street during traffic."

You want to get up. "I should sleep," you say.

Donald grabs you. "You're a fucking moron, Ricky."

"No, I'm not."

"You're like every other motherfucker in here."

You're thinking he's going to hit you. You get up but he just sits there with his hair in his eyes. "Why are you like the way you are?" you ask, but he doesn't talk now. You reach out to touch him, but you smack him instead, without even thinking, across the face. You hit him in the head, and arms, then on the chest. You're right up on him and both of your arms and hands are throbbing with the way it feels to touch him like this. You're on top and he's on the bed and you're trying to give him what he wants. He's yelling. He wants it to hurt. He wants it to hurt bad. He's covering his face and moving toward the wall and pretending. He's doing you a favor. He's saying you're crazy, someone help, you're fucking nuts. The door opens and the guard is saying, "Ricky, get off. Back up!" The guard is in the room and he's bending your arms behind you. He is pushing you out and holding your wrists against the middle of your back as he leads you into the long, loud hallway of men who are watching and whistling as you go by.

He takes you out of the cell block and into a room with pictures on the walls. There are chairs all around, like in a waiting area. Another guard drags one of the chairs toward the middle and handcuffs you to it. You're in there alone for a long time, sitting in the chair, with a fiery and disordered ache still in your arms and face. Every so often you can hear the sound of something mechanical, an engine of some kind on the other side of the wall. There are shelves filled with magazines and thick paperbacks, and a small window, high up, with a white curtain. It is different in here, not like the rest of the prison. It is for employees, you think. That you're handcuffed to the meager chair seems like a joke.

Eventually you hear the door, and the guard comes, with two little cups. "Here," he says. One of the cups is full of water, and the other has a pill in the bottom, something small and yellow, and unfamiliar. "I can't," you say. "I can't take it."

"Yeah, you can. It's fine." He sounds bored, like he's said this before. "I promise. Just swallow it. It's so you can sleep."

Stare at the pill, and then the guard. Recall the distant rapture of pharmaceuticals. "People get nervous, Ricky. You're a kid. Shit is scary. Take the pill."

Dump the pill out of the cup into your hand and put it in

your mouth. Drink the water and swallow. The guard says to stand up and come with him. He walks you out of the room, down another hall into a different cell where there's just a cot and a toilet. This is the hole. You know it once you're inside. The door is closed and then it's too dark to see. You feel your way around. The guard says he'll see you later. You find the cot and lie down and think about Nanny for a long time until, finally, you're seized by the miraculous buoyancy of the little pill. After that, there's not much.

There is a long corridor of solid metal doors that eventually open to the prison yard, and then to an enormous parking lot, and beyond that the grass and the interstate where the cars pass all day long like birds migrating in both directions. In the morning no one talks about what happened. They give you a bus ticket and eighty-six dollars. "For food," the man says, after he explains how long the trip will take, and the various stops, on the way back to Indiana. They give you the same clothes you were wearing when you came in. You don't know how to feel about this. It's like you're supposed to walk out and pick up where you left off. You sit down on the floor and tie your shoes. You have forgotten about them. You see them on your feet and you're shocked by the way they look.

A stocky lady wearing red lipstick and big sunglasses comes out from behind the desk she's sitting at and says, "Come on, Ricky. I guess I'm taking you." She talks into her radio. She says some numbers. You don't know what they mean. You follow her out of the door and to a car. You're not sure if you should open the car door yourself or wait for her to do it. She comes up behind you and puts her hand on your back and says, "You can sit up front—if you want."

You get in the front seat of the car. The interior is hot. It feels good against the backs of your legs. Go with her, down the service road, onto the interstate. It's a few miles to the bus stop, where there's a sign in the window that reads GIVE US YOUR HUNGRY, which seems very silly to you. This is not prison. This is a bus stop. Here the shoe meets the grass. After she drives off, you stand there for a long time. If you wanted you could stare down at the gravel parking lot all day. This is where people get up from their seats any time they want and maybe even walk to the North Pole if they think there's something there worth walking to. It smells like dirt, and the bitter exhaust of so many buses. You're like John Smith, you think, or William Clark, or Amerigo Vespucci, an eager frontiersman plodding off toward the darkest places.

This Is a Galaxy

When his father was only nineteen he moved to the United States from Turkey. The only things he brought with him were a black and green embroidered apron and a stolen library book titled *The Universe.* Some of the first words his father learned in English were words he'd read in the book. He sometimes used words from the book to describe random things: This or that was a supernova. A coworker was a black hole. The day's electromagnetic energy was off. A room had too much gravity. The neighbor's dog was a red dwarf. That guy at the deli, what a quasar.

Tamer sometimes pictured his father on an airplane wearing only the apron, holding the book in his lap. He had real memories too though. His father reading in bed, wearing his orange afghan like a cape. His father standing in front of the bathroom mirror, pulling his robe tight against his meager body while he sang along to Fleetwood Mac or Sezen Aksu, the queen of Turkish pop, sauntering demurely toward the mirror to give his reflection a little kiss.

Once, when he was maybe ten years old, Tamer used a box cutter and masking tape to make a flip-book out of the yearly portraits his father had taken of him at Sears. As the pictures flicked against his thumb he imagined how it might feel to grow up in an instant.

When Tamer tore the flip-book apart, his father asked, "What for? It was looking so good."

"I don't know," Tamer said. "I just wanted to." When Tamer stapled the pictures back together he put them in the wrong order, so that when he flipped through it again his face shifted between ages.

His father's bedroom was like the smallest antique store, with a high four-poster bed in the middle and two walls of shelves on either side where he displayed his things: polished stones, finger cymbals, daggers with naked ladies carved into the handles, a model of the space shuttle *Atlantis*, many postcard photos of Stevie Nicks. The two of them lay in bed facing opposite directions, their backs touching. It was warmer that way. The windows were drafty. Tamer asked his father about a giant telescope in Arizona, then about an elevator in Ukraine that a person could ride from a mountaintop overlooking the Black Sea, straight down through the mountain to the beach below.

Sometimes he'd say to his father, "Tell me about the time my mother disappeared in the cave on Mackinac Island and was never seen again." And his father would tell him the story, or if he was in a bad mood, he'd say, "I never took her to Mackinac Island. We have never been there with her. The caves are shallow. You could not lose a ladybug in them, much less a lady."

Other times, if he wanted to change the subject, his father would say, "I could tell one story about a summer in Afyon when moss covered the south side of every tree." If you looked down at the two of them from above the bed, Tamer imagined, it appeared as if he'd grown from his father's spine. He imagined himself as a small twin hanging there, his legs dangling even as his father walked around town, made the beds at work, riffled meticulously through the knickknack aisle at the St. Vincent de Paul thrift store.

His father sighed into the pillow. He said, "This is like baby. A ten-year-old should not always go to bed with the father. He should sleep on his own."

"You always say that, but I'm still here," Tamer said. "And I'm not tired, and you know what else?"

"You want to hear how I cannot hold open my eyes?"

"No, about the time the people in Turkey quit their jobs to burn corn, when you said they looked at the sky and knew they had to set the cornfields on fire."

"It was wheat," his father said.

Tamer pictured the bedroom ceiling unfolding like the lid of a giant box, revealing a vivid collection of stars above the house. He pictured his father being vacuumed into that far-off glitter. He pushed his feet beyond the length of the blanket and his father rolled over, burying his nose in Tamer's hair. When Tamer closed his eyes again, his father had drifted even farther away into outer space—a single mote floating through the constant black.

"Okay, Tamer, the day your mother died I was in line at a bank, waiting. This was on Poplar Street, which is downtown

Detroit. She was crossing Second Street. That was maybe two blocks from the bank we were at. I was cashing my paycheck and she was run over by a moving van."

Tamer sat up. "Before you said it was a limousine. What was I doing?"

"It was an eighteen-wheeler. You were crying for a Dum Dum. You know, also, the saddest part, the day before she died we had a terrible fight and she cracked my favorite Diana Ross album, *Silk Electric*, over her knee. Like a stick! I had to throw it in the trash! It was the very next day she died."

Tamer had no trouble talking to his father or to himself or to his father's friend, Philip Point, but around anyone else his mouth seized—a blip traveled toward the back of his throat and scattered, like a spark. The counselor at school called it a speech phobia.

"Oh, but at home you should hear his wonderful English," his father said to the counselor, misunderstanding the diagnosis. "He speaks as an adult!"

"Break your bread here, over the table or over the counter," his father said in the morning, "or don't break it at all and instead I will cut it in half for you with the bread knife if you will hand it to me. Let me see it."

"Put lots of butter on it and I'll eat it on the way to the bus stop," Tamer said.

"Look at you. Your shirt is inside out."

Tamer put his shirt on the right way and took the bread and walked down the street to the bus stop where the other children waited in their colorful jackets. He positioned himself just beyond the clutch of rowdy grade-schoolers and didn't speak. He stared down at the sidewalk, counting the cracks.

During the day his father worked at the Sunrise Motel on Chase and Ford as a housekeeper and desk clerk. In the classroom at Lakeside Primary, rummaging through a pencil box, Tamer felt dull and forgettable as a stone. During recess he paced the perimeter of the gymnasium. Each lap was a segment he could clip from the day, an hour scored into strips until there was nothing left, until a voice came over the garbled intercom, saying, "Bus seventeen riders please report to the north entrance."

There were times late at night when Tamer should have been asleep that he'd hear his father's music and go into the living room to find him curled up on the couch, wearing his special satin robe with the long braided belt, laughing and telling jokes with his friend Philip. Philip and Tamer's father would sometimes stare at each other for a long time, taking sips from the same bottle of Seagram's Seven until one of them turned to courteously exhale his cigarette smoke.

"Go into bed, Tamer," his father said at the sight of him in the hallway.

"I'm going to sleep with you," Tamer said.

"No, sir. Good night, please."

"Hello, Philip," Tamer said. "These pajamas are new. You can come in here and talk to me."

"No, he will not," his father said.

Philip and Tamer's father sat on the couch with their legs overlapping, smoke rising from the overfilled ashtray on the table, Perseus or Gemini lighting up the sky outside the long bay window behind the stereo cabinet. The house lights were out but the moon and the constellations shone into the living room as Tamer ran his fingers across the raised pattern of the wallpaper, heading slowly back down the hallway in the dark. In the other room his father and Philip would whisper and laugh, and the bottle would clink against the ashtray while the music played, until Tamer finally lay in bed long enough to reenter a dream—to cross from thinking to sleeping like a cloud thinning out in the sky.

Then there was a situation at the grocery store. It was close to dark and the temperature had dropped several degrees during the half hour they'd spent inside. This is how Michigan is. Two men inside of Food Pride followed Tamer and his father out to the parking lot. The tall one said, "Excuse me, ma'am, can we help with the groceries?" The heavy one laughed and a blast of breath rose from his mouth. They grabbed their crotches and blew kisses and the tall one said, "Listen, baby, what are you doing later? Where's your husband?"

"He's got lipstick on," the heavy one said, both of them erupting into a fit of laughter.

When they reached the car, his father said, "Shut up, both of you. There's a child in this backseat. Just go from here!"

But the tall one reached out, touching Tamer's father on the arm, saying, "No one gives a shit if we're out here, baby. You're in America now. We just wanna look at you." The man leaned forward, bringing his face in close as if he were about to kiss Tamer's father right on the lips. "Sexy faggot," he said, "I can't stop looking at you. I'm lost in your pretty eyes."

The heavy one was standing by, smiling, then not smiling. He watched Tamer sitting there in the backseat, holding the toy he'd gotten from the coin machine at the checkout. The heavy one coughed into the shoulder of his jacket, thrust his hands deep into the pockets. Tamer's father got into the car and slammed the door. When he started the engine and began to pull off, one of them smacked his hand hard against the roof, making a sound like thunder inside the vehicle.

In the backyard Tamer would assemble Erector sets, the structures eccentric and lopsided. He'd build them and take them apart, slipping unevenly, helplessly, toward adolescence.

One day a package arrived in the mail. "I waited for you to get here," his father said. It was from his aunt, his father's sister, in Afyon.

Years later Tamer would receive a letter too. He'd notice how the aunt's Turkish script crept into her written English the same way it had his father's, the barbed handwriting like black fingernail clippings thrown across the page. He'd hear his father in the letter, his voice with all its foreign blunders. Tamer would stand in the foyer of his apartment building, a grown man, facing the elevator. The elevator doors were old and wouldn't close all the way but the car kept going as he stepped forward, putting his hands on either side of the frame so he could lean in to gaze up at the elevator ascending into darkness. A bulb would flash, red, then dark again, filling the shaft like gas flooding a line. Partly it'd be the mechanism of the elevator, the tense roar of the engine, the pulsing light, the raw pink of dusk coming through the plate-glass doors behind him, all of it making it seem like every door could be a portal into the past, every opening a chink in time where he could swiftly pass into that long-ago living room to sit on the couch next to his father. There'd be music playing in one of the first-floor apartments, and a woman by the mailboxes pouring vodka into a soda bottle. Outside would be the sharp climate of near-spring in Detroit.

Before opening the package, his father had explained to him that in Afyon there were no yards to play in, just miles of cramped buildings and houses and a castle built high on a hill of volcanic rock in the center of the city, every brick road sloping toward the countryside. He told Tamer about the restaurant that was also a library, where he had stolen the book about the universe. "It was the only English book, hidden behind the others, but I like it most for the pictures." His father explained that on his nineteenth birthday he'd left the library with the book in his satchel, and how during the months that followed he'd applied for a passport, planning a trip to the United States with money an uncle had sent him on the condition he'd come to work at the uncle's motel until the debt was repaid. His father stayed working at the motel, even after the young American couple took it over and the uncle, claiming he was bored with the cheapness of Western lodging, returned to Turkey.

"Now we will open the mail! How exciting this is!" his father said, carefully getting at the box with a nail file, lifting out the contents and laying them on the table before Tamer as if he were presenting him with two precious heirlooms. Wrapped in orange tissue paper was a box of cookies and a videotape. There was a note attached to the video by a thick rubber band. His father read it aloud in Turkish, not even bothering to translate.

"Should we watch?" his father said.

"Okay," Tamer said, "and I'll eat the cookies?"

"Do you know what kind they are? They are special."

"So I can't eat them?"

"No, I was only saying they are special."

It was a grainy black-and-white recording. At the first sharp quivering of a clarinet, his father screamed, "Oh! It is Esma Redžepova singing 'Chaje Shukarije'!" He patted Tamer on the knee as they sat on the couch in front of the television, the light washing out his father's lean face. There was the long exhalation of an accordion, and a woman singing in a high, birdlike vibrato. Tamer's father sat still on the edge of the couch, mouthing every word, wiping his tears with the corner of his apron. In this moment Tamer felt his father was not his father but a stranger. The men on the videotape formed a circle around Esma Redžepova, swaying back and forth while playing their instruments, tilting in close to sing backup on the chorus. Tamer ate the cookies, which were crisp and rich, like sugared nuts, while his father stared dreamily. "What a stylish dance! This is a whole galaxy!" his father said. Esma Redžepova, with her many necklaces and round, serious face, was the first woman Tamer had ever looked upon and felt a kind of desire—a yearning to hold and examine entirely.

A dim cluster. A stolen library book. The slow excavation of a beginning. What is a memory? A sand-filled crater on the surface of one's most solid self? Decades later, Tamer would feel, each time he recalled something, the small, sad changes being made—like a hand disturbing a compact cavity of sand as he searched for the bottom.

By the time he was sixteen, stocky and disheveled, acne budding along his jaw, his hair unclean and long enough to hide behind, the once prolonged *M* and those manic repetitions at the start of words had been rubbed from his voice, leaving mostly silence in their place. He was just back from the neighbor's house and throwing his sneakers toward the sofa. He was holding a paper sack full of old *Hustler* magazines that the neighbor boy had sold him for four dollars. In the kitchen the rug was unraveling, gathering around the legs of the table and the metal chairs, running under the refrigerator. His father was laying down, wearing his apron and a purple Nike T-shirt, staring up at the ceiling fan. The video of Esma Redžepova played on the television in the living room. There was the usual furious pumping of the accordion, the shocking timbre of Esma's voice, and inside the music, a ringing, until he moved closer to the kitchen, so that all the colors of the room shifted and it was not the rug, but something soaking through his father's shirt and apron, spreading out like thick, dirty water across the linoleum. He went into the room. The floor was smeared with blood. He got down with a dish towel and pressed it against his father's chest. The blood soaked through. He grabbed all of the dish towels. He yelled, "Wake up right now, motherfucker!" He heard his voice in the room and it was not like his own voice but instead like his father's when he yelled at the neighbor's dog. It was a cheap sound. It was the heaviest thing. His father had already stopped breathing. Tamer thought his own throat was going to close shut too. He didn't want to leave the room to call the ambulance, but he made himself go to the phone. He pressed the towels one at a time until he found the exact place where the blood came from. It was a small hole. He could put a finger over it and make it disappear. He tore the flimsiest towels apart and tied a single long bandage around his father's chest. He sat there, holding the sticky towels in place, attempting a chaotic CPR until the paramedics came through the door and pulled him aside.

The suspects left tracks from the door to Selden Avenue, one block south. They took his father's shoes and pitched the gun, like litter, into a nearby drainage ditch.

"Why would they take his shoes?" Philip cried, hours later, after they'd left the police station. He pulled his car onto the shoulder of the Southfield Freeway, pounding his fists against the steering wheel. He couldn't stop crying. "Who are the police?" he asked Tamer. "Who am I? I am somebody. Who are they?" He was screaming it. "You can stay with me, Tamer!" Philip's face was bloated, as if injected with something, all of his features seized in fear.

Tamer stayed at Philip's house in Dearborn Heights. He lay on the couch, staring at the TV, eating mixing bowls full of cereal, hiding in the bathroom, watching reruns of *Family Matters* or *Step by Step* or *ER*. There was no funeral service. There wasn't enough money for one. Or else Philip couldn't pull himself together long enough to arrange it. Late at night, hours after Philip had drugged himself with sleeping pills, Tamer would jolt from a half-sleep, feeling as if he were being hauled viciously out of his own body—pulled into a black hallway, tugged under dark waters, dragged through a bottomless hole in the floor. Soon there was a wooden box on Philip's bedside table. Philip said, "What are we going to do?" But Tamer could only shrug and stare at the TV. A med student stepped away from a body. Dr. Doug Ross hovered with a scalpel. "Stop!" the visiting attendant said. "This lady is suffering from pulmonary edema!" Tamer would stand in Philip's room and stare at the wooden box until he thought Philip might come in, then he'd go back to the couch. Early in the mornings Tamer could hear Philip in the sunroom, his spoon clanking against a cup as Philip sobbed in the high, ugly tone of a teenage girl. Sometimes, Tamer could tell, Philip tried to hold it in his chest until it sounded like he was gagging. "Ejder, Ejder," he said. It was surprising to hear. It was as if Tamer's father didn't have a name until now, until Philip said it. Tamer could not bring himself to get up from the couch to go and comfort Philip. It didn't seem appropriate.

"I don't see any reason why you can't stay as long as you want and we'll see about getting your father's Oldsmobile over here so you'll have something to get around in. I know you'll want his car, unless you don't?" Tamer was sitting on the back porch, thinking he'd drive the awful car, and he could stay with Philip. He decided Philip was the only other person who loved his father and maybe he wouldn't mind being here with him. No one from Afyon called or wrote or came, though who, other than Tamer, could've told them what had happened? Philip and Tamer drove to the house on a Saturday and Tamer filled some boxes with all the things he wanted to take. He didn't look in the kitchen. The body was somewhere else. The body was suspended in time. The kitchen was clean as a tooth. They left the house and locked the doors and Philip gave Tamer the keys, dropped them into his palm on the porch. They planned on coming back in a week for his father's car, but instead the police came to Philip's house, with a social worker, saying Tamer had to appear in court. Philip had it all wrong, he said to Tamer, he wasn't thinking.

They took Tamer in the back of the police car to a children's home where he slept on a cot at the foot of another bed. The next day he sat with a judge in a cramped office while the social worker read aloud from a folder of papers. Afterward, alone together in the men's room, Philip asked Tamer whether he understood what was happening. Tamer said he did not.

"I don't think I do either. I've been too upset. You'll be eighteen soon, though," he said, "and we can sort it all out."

"That's more than a year from now," Tamer said.

Philip washed his hands at the sink and dried them. He stared at his shoes. He said, "I wonder if someone is wearing the shoes? Do you think someone's wearing them?"

"How would I know?" Tamer said, the heat draining from his body all at once. He turned away from Philip's lifeless face in the mirror and headed toward the door.

Philip drove Tamer to the foster family's house but wouldn't get out of the car. Tamer walked to the steps to meet the social worker, who smiled while handing him her card and a piece of candy. "Their names are Patsy and Darryl," she said, "and their daughter's name is Cecelia." Tamer didn't turn around when Philip drove off. Instead he stared at the obnoxious wreath hanging on the front door, trying not to drop the heavy box he was holding.

They wanted to shake his hand. They wanted to take him out in the backyard to show him the basketball hoop. His room had a single bed and a large metal desk. They emptied the closet so he could put his things inside.

During the first days he ate his meals at the desk. The Buckleys used paper plates. They used plastic forks and plastic cups. It was hard being in the house. He felt paralyzed by the pressure to speak. In the afternoons, when the house was still empty, he went into the living room to watch television. He would come out of his room at night to sit on the couch and watch *ER*. Cecelia said *ER* was boring but Patsy called it "a high-octane drama!" "We love it, don't we Tamer?"

Pasty was loud and looked, always, as if she'd just returned from vacation. Her skin was flushed and bronzed, and her clothes seemed suited for someone much younger.

Twice he put on the videotape of Esma Redžepova. He mouthed some of the words. He looked at the black-and-white footage and wondered how she must look—aged, or different now, not the slight, agile woman on the videotape.

Tamer called Philip once a week, just for the chance to speak without having to dislodge every word like a seed from a straw. "Are they treating you nice?" Philip asked. "Do you talk?" Tamer didn't respond, which, of course, was his answer. When he closed his eyes he felt that every new movement he made left a blur, every new instance of stillness a bright orb. It was as if he were tracking himself, like a satellite.

In the courthouse the judge had asked Philip, "What is your relationship to the father? You were friends?"

"We were friends," Philip said.

But it didn't feel like the truth to Tamer. What else could he have said? It was like he was being interviewed for a job he didn't want. He touched his face too many times, ran his fingers inside the cuff of his pant leg and repeated the questions back as if they were impossible to answer.

Darryl Buckley owned a butcher's shop and said to Tamer, "If you want some extra spending money you could come and work after school or on the weekends."

Darryl and his wife stared at each other from across the dinner table. Patsy looked at Tamer but spoke to Darryl, saying, "Tell him what time to come to work."

"After school, Patsy. I already said that."

"He did," said Tamer.

Cecelia fished a bone from her mouth, laid it on the edge of her paper plate. "I'm sorry," she said, "it's a bone." Her hair was careful and made her look like an adult. She wore ugly clothes too. "Business casual," she called it. Patsy and Cecelia both had large, glassy eyes like cartoon forest animals and together consumed many packages of chocolate almonds.

"I'm glad you're eating with the family, Tamer," Cecelia said. It sounded as if she had rehearsed it.

Tamer longed for a moment like the one on the video, where the camera panned to capture an overhead view of all the musicians in their huddle, their heads nearly touching as if they were spokes attached to some hidden axis, their large gauzy shirts brushing against each other as they rose up and leaned back to reveal Esma Redžepova. She lifted her arms above her head, twirled her wrists and splayed her fingers. She turned to look at the camera while the men swayed and circled her, like many moons moving into alignment. "Hello, Esma. Hello, many moons," Tamer said to himself in the living room, unsettled by the sound of his own voice. The whole scene, with its perfect choreography, made him even more desperate for his father, for the now-lost moments in his life when every action was carried out with grace and inherent rhythm.

He was sitting alone with Patsy in the kitchen in his new basketball shorts when she reached over to put a hand on his leg, running her finger up his thigh. "You're a beautiful man, Tamer. I bet your father was a beautiful man. Are all Turkish men so handsome? You want to help me bread the fish?"

"No," he said, getting up from the table and walking out into the yard. He stood behind the garage, watching bees swarm an empty soda can.

In the butcher shop he stocked the shelves and ran the register until Darryl came in one afternoon with a set of knives he'd bought especially for Tamer. "I appreciate them," Tamer managed to say. There was a chart in the back room showing the animals and all their parts. Tamer stared gravely at it when there was nothing else to do. He would arrange and rearrange the animal parts on the cutting table. He made the cuts along the meat, and each time the effort of his hand holding the knife seemed to lessen, or soften, so that eventually it felt as if every animal were designed to be disassembled. Darryl fried pork skins in the deep fryer and complained about the customers. Other times he hid in the office doing crossword puzzles. At the end of every week he paid Tamer his hourly wage and occasionally a little more. "To save," he said, leaving Tamer to close up alone.

Eventually he made Tamer shoot a cow. They drove to a meat locker in Hamtramck. Tamer watched as a man in rubber coveralls put a gun against a cow's head. The man gave the gun to Tamer and explained how to use it. He took Tamer's hand in his own and pressed the barrel to the hair between the cow's gelatinous eyes. Tamer pulled the trigger. The handgun made a quick, dull pop and after the slaughter Darryl explained how to dig the bullet from the brain. Tamer pushed a finger into the tepid smoothness, excavating a tiny shell.

He felt dislodged.

Cecelia found a dead cat on the carport and asked Tamer if he would help her bury it. "It's the right thing to do," she said, her hand perched insincerely on her hip. He couldn't help but wonder, too often now, what Cecelia looked like without her clothes on. The girls in his class were quiet or else they shrieked manically at one another from across the lunch table. While Cecelia was looking for a shovel Tamer put his mouth up to the cat's and blew.

"Disgusting!" she said, coming around the corner of the garage. "You're crazy! You're going to catch a feline disease." He looked at her in her elaborate sweater, a dire expression on her face. He looked back down at the cat. It lay there stiff as a doll. Wouldn't it be something, he thought, if the cat began to squirm?

After dark he went into the yard again. He'd been lying in bed just thinking about the cat. He was still in his underwear, and he knelt down beside the small grave. He brushed the dirt away. Move a leg, move anything, he thought. It felt as if so much time had passed—he was so different, he thought, each day. How long, he wondered, would that feeling last? It was as if time were passing too quickly and also not at all.

As he was falling back asleep his father came and stood at the foot of the bed. He opened his satin robe and showed Tamer his chest. His lungs looked waxy and crooked inside the open, raw cavity. His father slowly turned his head toward the bedroom door, then even slower back to Tamer. It was as if he was trying to say something. He had a guilty, exhausted expression. Finally, in a voice that wasn't familiar, his father said, "That was a nice thing to do, for the girl, Tamer."

"Thank you," Tamer whispered back.

Tamer had sex with Patsy Buckley on the Fourth of July while Darryl and Cecelia were at the levee watching fireworks. She asked him again, "Are all Turkish men like this?"

"I don't know," he said.

"You're a virgin?" she said.

"Yes," he said.

"I don't give a shit," she told him. "I deserve this. You deserve this. Look at me while you're inside me so I can see your beautiful face."

They were in the garage, in the backseat of the car. What he wanted to do, but was afraid to, was lower himself down to where he entered her, to examine the secret shapes of her body, to see how it all worked. But the whole situation felt involuntary and embarrassing, so he kept his eyes closed and allowed her to do most of the work.

He understood that his mother had left them all those years ago because she was living with a man who didn't need her, a man who couldn't help but stare at other men while waiting in line at the grocery store, the filling station, the park. His father loved to cut the sandwiches into triangles and wipe the bathroom mirror and steam the cushions on the couch—he adored steaming the cushions. Tamer wondered if all mothers were like Patsy Buckley, hiding out in their garages at night with their rum and cokes, reading ragged copies of *The Thorn Birds* or *Kaleidoscope* until their husbands fell asleep watching television in bed.

Tamer lived with the Buckleys for a year and three months. He moved out two weeks after his eighteenth birthday. They had a party for him in the backyard. The smell of charcoal clung to their clothes, the icing slipped off the cake. Patsy spilled a daiquiri down the front of her sundress and sat with it dripping between her breasts. She insisted they sing "You Are My Sunshine" instead of "Happy Birthday." He quit working at Darryl's shop and used the money he'd saved to rent an apartment in Southfield. He got a job at Leonard's Meat Processing on Nine Mile Road and for the first time ever he was alone.

There's a rainbow sheen in certain cuts of meat. Tear it from the bone, hold it up to the window. Sometimes when light hits a side of beef it splits into colors. At Leonard's there was a system

51

of tracks along the ceiling of the locker so that the cows and pigs could be rotated and spun, like clothes on a rack. He could tear down a full-grown hog in less than an hour. He'd slide a bucket under the hog where it hung from the ceiling like a colossal coat. The blood spun down. The organs plopped. Hardly anyone talked to him. The hog bled what little blood it had left and the bucket filled to the lip or overflowed onto the floor.

Tamer would not have said he was lonely, but he pulled a milk crate up to his living room window after dark so that any-one on the street could see him sitting by himself. Outside Detroit hummed like a hundred faraway motorboats. He shaved his face and washed his body at the kitchen sink. He looked at the skyline on his walk to work in the mornings, watched the sunlight spread like a spill, watched the city soak it up like a rag.

Philip came by, eventually, with an old reclining chair. In Tamer's new apartment he emptied a bag of curtains onto the floor, insisting they should hang them up. "Everyone can see in," he said. He stood on the cushion of the unsteady chair and clipped the hooks over the rod. "My God," he said, "you're so high up." Tamer brought two beers from the refrigerator and they drank them on the living room floor. "You shouldn't have these," Philip said, appearing uneasy and out of reach.

"I know," Tamer said, "but the clerk at the liquor store is Turkish. I wanted a reason to say hi."

"You could have bought a soda," Philip said. "Did you talk to him?"

"No," Tamer said. "And I wanted these."

The fluorescent light in the kitchen blinked off and on and

after a while Philip said he had to go. Tamer put his hand on Philip's shoulder in the doorway, the way he'd seen other grown-ups do. Moments later he watched from the window as Philip got into his car and pulled out into the intersection. Tamer stood at the window with the new curtains wide open, watching the city grow dark. He could see Philip with his turn signal flashing as he moved out of sight. Across the street was another row of apartment buildings with the balconies lit up. If he leaned close enough to the glass he could make out the edge of Bouveric Woods, a tight mass of trees with limbs like many arms broken and healed incorrectly.

Tamer had come to a place where he could at least imagine what he might say to Philip or to anyone he wanted to talk to, even if he couldn't yet say the things aloud. He thought he'd like to say, "It's hard to stop being angry that he's not around. It's hard to stop thinking about him all the time," or "I don't know how to stop wanting him around for no good reason other than to have him here." He wanted to ask, "How much longer will it be like this?" even though he knew the answer was probably forever.

He worked, or watched television, or practiced saying simple things to strangers. He stood in the foyer of his apartment building watching the people on the street. He waited by the elevator as if he were about to meet someone, as if any minute a conversation might begin. It was late summer when he received the letter from his aunt. The address was only partial, and she had misspelled the name of the city. In the letter she explained how she had learned about his father's death through the manager at the motel, that months afterward the family had held a small service of their own in Afyon and how she wished Tamer could have been there. The aunt said she would someday like to visit him in "Destroy." Outside two older gentlemen took each other's hands and stepped off the curb, beginning a slow walk across the street. The radio in the first-floor apartment went off, and the woman in the chair poured more vodka into her soda bottle. Tamer waved to her and quickly turned back toward the elevator. He wanted to step through the doorway and into his old house.

Philip had never offered him the wooden box, but it didn't matter. What he really wanted was to return to the house with a box cutter and remove the rectangle of linoleum where his father had died. It was something he thought of often. He played it over in his head, drawing out the plot, precisely cutting through the material and peeling back the slick sheet so he could roll it up like a scroll. That was the moment. It was the last place his father had been, the last place he'd touched. He wanted to reach through the open elevator doors and into the kitchen, to find that smaller version of himself making a picture book, to hear the accordion bellows unpleat and watch his father dance to the music before lying down on the kitchen floor. It was strange hearing a song that many times and not knowing what it meant beyond the meaning he had made for it. He would put the picture book on the table and lie down on the floor too. He'd ask his father for another story about his mother and it would be the truth this time. His father would sit up and look at him or lay his head gently on Tamer's stomach, pressing his ear in close. He'd have said something like, "Wait. I think I can hear something in there, Tamer. In your belly," or "Hold, please. This is radio waves from space! It is from stars colliding. The noise has been traveling all these years from another, distant planet. And just now it has arrived." Tamer could imagine almost anything his father might say. He could arrange the words and his father would be there for a minute, in a lonely, consoling way. It was getting harder, though, to hear the actual voice, to feel the deep presence that was only possible because of the sounds he made when he spoke, no matter what the words meant. He wasn't sure how he was supposed to feel about this, angry or lucky, that someday the sound of his father's voice might be gone for good.

In Motel Rooms

There were hidden microphones in all the motel rooms where my husband stayed, not just at Harbourview. Bugs, they called them, transmitters attached to a bed frame or light fixture or some other place we'd never find. I'd start to converse about some personal matter and Martin would say, Baby, wouldn't it be nice to have a record player in here, and I'd know to change the subject, we were being recorded. Most times I didn't go with him. I was at the reading in South Carolina because it was his birthday and the children were with my brother, Obie, in Tuscaloosa. The motel room was full of people, friends who'd come to hear Martin read. He'd had his second book published. Albert and I got Martin a cake at the last minute. Clara came in with all the candles lit, smiling awfully sly at Martin while she sang "Happy Birthday." I loved singing with them. They all sounded so good. Martin had gotten his hair cut and was wearing a sharp blue suit. I was sad the children couldn't be there. It was strange that with them I felt suffocated, but when I was away I just ached, I thought about their screaming and running and soft faces. The weather was unusually warm, the middle of winter and nearly seventy degrees. Martin laughed a lot and I stood to the side, near an open window with the curtains blowing against my legs.

Even after everyone left, the room still felt full, with all the windows up and the sounds of the harbor coming in. The rooms were usually clean but I'd tidy them anyway, wipe down the furniture and sink and tub. I would put all the clothes in the drawers, even for a night. A motel is not like any house, Lord knows. I wondered if the squeaking of the wet rag on the porcelain sink was picked up by the microphones. I thought back to all the things that happened in the room that day, the singing and the preaching and the sound of me unpacking and of me talking to myself just before I started cleaning. All of it was recorded.

This was around the same time my hands had started to ache from what was arthritis, though I didn't know it yet. They started hurting that night while I put on my lipstick. This is strange, but if I sat on them they would feel better and the energy there would stop. I sat on my hands in the motel room in South Carolina before I put on my earrings. Martin was going to read from his book, and I'd brought a copy with me, a fine hardback edition. The paper had a rich smell. I liked to hold it, run my fingers over the pages. In the conference room of the Harbourview Inn, I sat beside Martin while he read at a podium. The room was warm and we were all perspiring, but the tables were set very nicely with carnation centerpieces, the cheapest of flowers, but still. Even though I'd heard and read the chapter a dozen times I smiled and felt charged up by it. Everyone was shouting and clapping and making him wait a minute for them to settle down. The chairs had been neatly arranged around the tables at first, but people began to stand up and move away from their seats like something had come over them. It was always like that, not like he was giving a speech or reading from a book but like it was Sunday worship. He gave different versions of the same speech many times but it was always like a brand-new thing that had just come to him, like a singer gives birth to a song no matter how many times it's been sung. I sensed that people never before thought the things Martin was saying. They'd been waiting their whole lives for my husband and didn't even realize it. The place was on fire. My own heart, I should say, was also lit by the cause.

THAT NIGHT IN our room, after the hand shaking and questions, I wrapped my head in a scarf and lay down. Martin went into the bathroom to pray. He closed the door and asked God to please deliver us and show him how to suck the venom. I'll put my mouth over their wounds, he said, draw out the venom and spit it into the everlasting waters. The radiator buzzed beneath the window but I could make out nearly every word. Take me there, show me how, he said. A knock came from the bathroom door, and I said, Yes, Martin? But he didn't answer. I opened my mouth to speak again but another voice came from inside the bathroom. Come in, Martin said. I could not move. The other voice echoed, as if spoken from the far end of a tunnel. I could feel it in my spine. The room lit up with the headlights of a car going down the little road beside the motel and the second voice filled the bathroom like a long hum with another, deeper sound inside it. I knew, somehow, that it was God.

For so long it was only in motel rooms with my husband that I could have dreams and remember them. They were always the same. Martin would pray and I would close my eyes and listen and begin to think of myself as a strip of unexposed film inside a movie camera. In the bed with my eyes closed I was plastic and dark, held securely by the spools, waiting to begin my revolutions before the lens of the camera.

I could count the days in a year Martin stayed in our house. I remained in Montgomery while he traveled the country. He'd made public his thoughts about the war and bought a new record player for our living room, partly as a gift, but also to say our house was infested too. We had several Mahalia Jackson albums. In the afternoons, with the children off at school, I would put on one of the records and sing the harmony. My sister called to say she saw my husband on the television. Who would have thought, she said, it would be our very own family in the center of all this? I said we had to make sacrifices, but didn't it feel good, sister? Didn't it make her feel alive? She said yes but it was also terrifying. Once she called and said she had a rash and I felt embarrassed. Not because it mattered about the rash, but because there was someone listening. I said, Edythe, mind what you say and then she got uncomfortable and hung up the phone.

In a briefcase under our bed, inside a copy of *Nobody Knows My Name*, there was a color photograph of a naked woman. Martin wouldn't have meant for me to see it. You could look at our room with its antique bed and never know that underneath was a photo of a naked white woman posing on an ugly yellow sofa. I had hundreds of envelopes to sort through. The phone rang all the time. One afternoon Dexter picked up the down-stairs line before I got to it and the operator said, Please get your child off the phone, the president of the United States is calling. I'd wake up before the sun and prepare the children's breakfast and hope every day that no one threw a bottle of gasoline across the front porch.

Montgomery to Memphis is three hundred miles in less than forty minutes. The airport there was surrounded by trees. I stepped out of the airplane and felt as if I'd arrived from the future. One minute I was in Montgomery, gathering things up around the house, saying goodbye to the children and Edythe and the next I was in Memphis. I'd decided to attend a Baptist convention. Martin worried about my coming with him. He said, Coretta, baby, people see the two of us together and they won-der who's home with the children. I was sure they did not. There was always something to be done. Our room had three tele-phones, all of them connected, Martin said, to the Federal Bureau of Investigation. I sat alone at the little table-and-chair set by the window and pictured wires strung up in the walls, miles of them like veins fed into a distant room where someone else sat, listening every minute for a clue. Ralph, Billy, Al, even Samuel showed up to help, bringing letters and newspapers and food. A boy in Yazoo City was found sealed up in a barrel of oil, drowned to death inside. I knew Martin would always be gone. I had to cover my face with my scarf. I stared out the window to keep the men from seeing. They went to dinner with some clergy from the Memphis Baptist Church and I stayed behind, eventually lying down on the bedspread even though the sun was still up. I rested alone in the dusky room until I had an awful dream where I had to drink glasses of crude oil. The sludge dripped down my chin and wrists and between my fingers. It stained my dress, which was pale green. In the dream I loved the dress. Several white women were there. They were saying, No, Ms. Scott, that's not the right way to drink it, don't swallow, inhale, breathe it in. They held the glass and tried to show me how to suck the oil into my lungs. I knew why they were saying my maiden name. It was hard to make myself breathe in the oil. It didn't make sense why I couldn't do it. The white women were very good at it.

Martin came back alone and brought me a plate of some good dumplings with corn on the cob. It was nice, just sitting there with him. In the neighboring room someone turned on Elvis Presley and I sang along while Martin and I played gin rummy on the bed. Martin laughed at my knowing all the words but I won the hand. I could smell the cigarette smoke of whoever had occupied the room before us. Martin fell asleep with his clothes on, not even going into the bathroom first to pray. After a while I could hear the voice calling but Martin just slept. There was a ticking sound, something spinning, like an old electric fan. Martin turned on his side and held the pillow against his chest. I stared at his mouth. His features looked fresh, like a child's. The ticking went on until a hum, like wind over a bottle, grew so loud I had to sit up and turn on the lamp. I waited for it to stop. It went on for a long time but finally I was in the twilight of sleep where again I could imagine myself as a strip of film, and I was thankful for that. I saw Martin's figure beside me, the dresser and nightstand, the suits on their hangers like men lined up against the wall. Over by the door there was a woman standing, watching. There was a sudden, unsettling stillness, as if she'd interrupted something. In my mind I could hardly make out Martin's face in the dark, but the woman's white skin stood out in the room like a clouded-over moon.

At home I slept and felt empty. Early in the morning I would hear things outside and think a crowd was gathering, but it was just the garbage truck or some child riding a bicycle with a tin can wedged between the wheel and fender. Sometimes Dexter and Bernice would hold hands all day if I let them. If Dexter fell asleep in his own bed at night he would reach out for his sister. The two eldest and the two youngest paired together for everything: Boy, girl. Boy, girl.

In July the mailman brought a package. I was excited because it was heavy, and important looking. I took it into the office and cut it open. Inside was another box, and a note that read: *You know what to do.* I went around looking out the windows and locking the doors. I went back into the office and locked that door too. Inside the second box were cassettes and a little black player. I knocked over my water glass trying to get it out of the box. The water ran off the desk and onto the floor but I just left it there and sat on my hands for a minute. On the tape was Martin's voice and the voice of a woman. I could tell she was white by the way she talked. There was an envelope with a typed transcript.

Ice in a glass?

Martin: You say you think she'll be fired now?

Female: (Laughing) I'm sure of it. Don't you think so?

Martin: Uh-huh.

Female: She was out of line and so was he.

Martin: Are you done yet?

Female: Almost. Goodness. (Unclear) I just feel better now that he knows I wasn't lying.

Martin: I understand. You shouldn't be working there.

Female: You're telling me. (Water running?) How do you always get me so calm?

Martin: I'm happy to. Lord, you look good right now.

Female: (Laughing) Do I?

Martin. Mmm-hmm. (Unclear)

Female: (Unclear)

Martin: Do you want to be (Unclear)?

Unidentifiable sounds.

After several minutes the woman on the tape started moaning. Martin said, Such a sweet thing, such a lovely thing, I'm happy you showed. There was heavy breathing. The bed made noises and the two said other things. More moaning. The children knocked at the door. What are you doing in there? Yoki said. Open the door, Mother, we're all trying to do the same thing and only two can play and Bernice is cheating. Okay, I told them, I'll be out, but instead I just sat there thinking that somewhere the FBI was listening to me right then. The children yelled again. Who's in there? they said. I was playing this tape of

Martin and the woman, and the FBI was recording me as I listened. I imagined someday listening to that tape too, like holding
a mirror up to another mirror. Martin asking, Are you done yet?
Woman laughing. Woman moaning. Martin saying, I'm happy
to. Unidentifiable sounds. Children yelling. Someone knocking
on the door saying, Mother, come out. Woman saying, You
always get me so calm. Other woman saying, Okay, I'll be there
in a minute, please stop.

It wasn't just that we were apart all the time. Of course he
made me feel loved. In our bed he would put his hand behind
my head and look me in the eyes. There is something to be said
about being looked directly in the eyes. Something would go off
in me, like a pistol report. There is desire in commitment. Over
all the years I was rising and falling. It was just like that. I don't
know how else to say it. Many men who said they were friends
of our family were certainly only friends to the cause. They
would stand outside of the motel rooms while my husband laid
his hands on these women, his fingers in their smooth, pale hair.
My husband's eyes were always wet. It was just the way he
looked. People always thought he was about to cry, though
he wasn't.

In late March I flew to Chicago for the weekend. Martin was
waiting for me at the gate. He held me and I pressed my face into
his jacket. He smelled like musk and starch. Some of the people in
the airport turned to stare, while others just walked right past.

There's always a threat, Al said to everyone at dinner that
night. We were at the home of Ralph and Wanda Jackson and
the talk of the evening was how there were those of secret

intelligence and those in the government. I had a hard time knowing the difference. I said to everyone, it is as if the FBI wants to study us, like we're animals and they're trying to learn something by subjecting us to constant surveillance. Coretta, Ralph said, in many ways you are wiser than all of us. Martin patted my leg. Either way, Martin said, they mean to keep a close watch or, God save us, eradicate people entirely, but those things have to be done outside of the law. Some of the men in government, they honored my husband. Others did not. While I was coming back from the restroom, Wanda stopped me in the hallway and put her arms around me. She held me for a long time. I did not know her as well as some of the other wives, and the light was out, making it hard to see, but I knew she was crying, so I hugged her back. She said, Coretta, I wish you'd think to call me sometime, you know us ladies have two sets of troubles, our own and everyone else's. After a while I told Martin I was tired and wanted to go. We rode back to the motel without saying much.

In the motel room in Chicago, Martin hung his suit and washed his hands at the sink while I put on my nightgown. He closed the bathroom door and asked that he might be allowed to go up to the mountain. He asked the Lord to please show him. I lay down in the bed and switched off the lamp. He said, I know you know about the threats and either allow them to stop or else make me unafraid. The vent kicked on and I heard a door open. There was the creaking of a hinge, but with words buried beneath it, like someone talking in a small, crackling voice. Someone was whispering from inside the bathroom, not Martin but a double voice. I wanted to call out, but instead I kept my eyes shut. Martin said, I am hungry, and so are they. What do we do, what do we say to the God of History? I waited for a long time but the sound of the opening doors went on and on until Martin said, Can I see the Promised Land?

When he came out and lay down beside me, he kissed me on the shoulder. I did not open my eyes to look at him. I lay there and thought, You are just a man, Martin, beside me on a bed. You're safe and tired, and what is fear but another, abnormal gift from the Lord Jesus Christ? I thought of the white women waiting on either side of us like security guards and how it felt to be in a room with my husband and know we were being recorded even as we drifted to sleep. I wanted all of the tapes the FBI had made, so I could put them together in order and hear what went on in the rooms when I wasn't there and so Martin could hear what went on in our house. He and I could listen to the whole thing together. I thought of the sounds, and the strange films I imagined in the twilights of sleep. I wondered why I was so inclined to combine the two, and why I also wished to look back years later and know that in most ways our efforts had matched, that they lined up, like two mirrors facing each other in a very long but narrow room.

Nettles

Of course the husband was mean. Back then all the husbands were. They moved out of the city on a whim, mostly his, to live on a seedy triangle of acreage in the country. Some important considerations regarding their marriage:

1. He'd built their little house in the city himself, supposedly for her, back in the earliest days when even those central-most municipalities were still developing. It was a metropolis on the verge: sporadic clutches of tall, redbrick factories and rows of shotgun houses. Theirs was one of the city's first modest bungalows. The husband and wife were from a time before the crime and fast-food chains. The bungalow was beautifully serviceable, with three small bedrooms and rich pine cabinetry all the way to the ceiling, complete with peculiar hinges and special compartments. She would go back into the city with a lady friend, twenty years later, on a doctor's visit, searching out a diagnosis for a rare blood disorder that would nearly end her life at forty-one. She'd never seen the ocean, but returning to that city again after living so long among gaping fields and farms, she felt lost at sea. An

electric sea. She felt mangled by the chaos of the freeways and its inexplicable, spiraling constructions. The place was made flashy and metallic and of questionable, compound materials so oddly arranged she could not make sense of it. She found her little house with an emaciated, brown-skinned lady in a denim miniskirt leaning against the porch post, sucking on an orange popsicle. The deep sucking of the popsicle riveted her. The porch lady gave them the finger as she and the friend waved from the passenger seat of their air-conditioned sedan. What had become of those smooth, naturally stained cabinets, she wondered? Her hand-crafted lazy Susan? Her lady friend, a retired prison guard, responded by saying, "You think every house without clean shutters is a crack house." Which was true.

2. The husband was great with the children, at first. Very attentive, slapstick in his comedy, always patiently instructing, right up until the children reached puberty, after which he ignored them like mangy strays. Was it their transformed genitals? the wife often wondered.

3. The husband's first wife was a lesbian, who he was still in love with and likely always would be.

He'd responded to an ad in the newspaper. *Rural home with finished attic on eight acres. 5000 sq feet animal processing facility on premises.* Prior to becoming a carpenter, he'd been a meat man. He'd loved being a meat man. Hacking into things soothed him. He could slice a steak thin as paper in seconds. Unless you ran the place, though, and slaughtered the animals yourself, there was no real money in it. He belonged to a middle-class generation of men who felt duped by capitalism, tossing at night on their too-soft mattresses, dumbfounded by the constant expansion between their labor and the fey furnishings slowly filling their homes. No amount of wrinkle-proof slacks or electric razors or frozen dinners could wipe the deep memory of bailing hay from his muscles. Once he saw the ad, that was it, he was a goner. She was fine with it, really. She was born to be a business owner, she decided, having thought it over for a day. Being a mother wasn't so easy. She could cook (bacon grease, Worcestershire), organize coupons, keep immaculate record books, darn, polish silver. Domesticity was a contest she was always winning. Except for the part about the children. She expected them to behave like miniature adults and was too desperate for their affection. It was difficult, having a husband who was in love with a dead lesbian. She'd kiss the children for too long, and requested many topless back rubs. She encouraged long, intertwined naps on the sofa from which the children awoke to find their mother's housedress hiked around her plump waist. Also she beat them too often. Mostly for being loud or complaining or playing in the drainage ditch. Of course he beat them too, but that was expected. A woman beating her children implied a hysterical lack of control. With a man it implied the opposite.

He put their city house on the market, emptied the savings account, and took out a sizable business loan from a locally owned bank in the new county. He went on ahead of them to ready the estate. During that time they spoke only once, when he called for instructions on how to poach an egg. His absence delighted and terrified her. Two weeks later he sent for them and the furnishings. Oh, weren't they an excited bunch, crossing the bridge out of the city, waving goodbye to the neon telephone company sign beside the river, finding themselves quickly in farm country, a few hours and there it was, the little town with a dusty candy store and one restaurant and an old abandoned movie theater with a dead marquee that read FOR SALE, and their new house, of course, out on the edge of everything, with a water well and a dozen birch trees and an actual broken-down combine rusting away in their very own pasture.

The slaughterhouse was a lengthy cinder-block building with tangled, flowering weeds growing around it. While the movers and the children unloaded all the furniture, she began pulling the plants with a sweaty, ravenous intensity. In her good shoes. And her black slacks and silk blouse and red fedora. "This building will have to be painted! Most likely multiple coats!" she informed her husband from across the new yard, as he lumbered grumpily up the porch steps with his fireproof lockbox. Turned out the weeds were poisonous nettles—tall and leafy with a tuft of white petals on top and invisible hairs down the stalk, like microscopic hypodermic needles. Her husband got a good laugh out of this, while she lay about wrapped in wet rags, squawking in agony on the sofa.

The next night they had sex on the attic floor while the children slept on a pile of linens downstairs. He'd not wanted to do it, but she insisted it was customary, so he lowered his pants to his ankles and pulled his briefs to the side. She lay there panting hungrily beneath him with a broad, closed-lipped smile on her face that reminded him of a pink balloon stretched tight, ready for inflation.

SOME THINGS THEY found that were curious about the country:

1. Strangers asked a lot of questions, questions that strangers in the city would never ask and couldn't care less to know the answer to. Rural folks would ask something and then start talking even before you'd finished responding. This was something she did herself. Though how in the hell had no one returned that simple disrespect before now? "Oh, that's just like me and my . . ."

"What a self-centered world we've found ourselves in," she said to her husband after those first few days around town.

He almost choked on his soup. "You've met your match," he said.

And she had.

2. The wife made so many friends she had a list of customers to fill an address book before they'd even opened for business. Just hearing about her friendly industriousness gave him a nosebleed and excruciating gas. He'd assumed he would smoke his own bacon and everyone would smell it and come driving over, that he'd open the building doors and people would file in to sample his cracklins. Maybe the men would want to chat about wildlife or war and he'd quickly demonstrate his breadth of knowledge on the subjects. Maybe a lady would smile at him, as he suggestively carved away at the luminous red flesh of a healthy beef.

3. The previous owners seemed gravely invested in the continued success of the business. They were an older couple who dressed with a painful and thrifty formality, in gray and brown synthetics. It wasn't that the couple didn't smile, it was that a serene pride rested beneath their stuffy manners, and also that the moment their antique pen was lifted from the document they'd procured from their ratty briefcase, the lady said, "You'll come to our service, then, on Thursday?"

"We will?" the wife said, too loudly, she realized.

"Sure!" the lady said. "Were you considering another church?"

"I guess we hadn't thought about that, had we?" the husband said.

"There's nowhere else you'll want to go," the lady assured them, her face wrung up like a rag. The lady sat at the kitchen table, compulsively sliding her palms down the dress, flattening the polyester over her expansive thighs.

"We'll think about it," the wife said to her husband. "Won't we?" And then, turning to the couple: "We'll let you know."

"Now, I want to warn you, because you seem like good people," the man said. "You've got some perverse elements living across the way, sexual deviants, men who lie with men, women who make congress with women! A bad lot."

"Is that the case?" the husband said, pulling a Lucky Strike from the pack on the table. He slid it between his yellowed fingers and put it up to his mouth where his upper lip had begun to twitch. When chewing tobacco wasn't nearby, he smoked, and as he lit the cigarette he sent an accusing glare at his wife, reprimanding her for any thoughts she might be having regarding the kinky neighbors. "We appreciate the heads-up," he said, nodding at the three of them before disappearing into the bathroom. "Pardon me," he said.

"It's a lovely church house," the man said. "Nicest one around here, ain't it, Louise?"

"Yes, sir," the lady said. Her hair was gray and dry as dirt, the ample mass piled on her head like a bristly cloud stabbed through with a dozen copper pins.

"Do you all want coffee or tea?" the wife asked.

"No thank you," the couple said, in a chilly, throbbing tandem. Their voices fit neatly inside each other's, making a single, fluttering sound that stunned the wife.

"We better be going, hadn't we?" the man said, standing up.

The lady agreed, following him out of the kitchen and onto the side porch, where they disappeared from sight, closing the door softly behind them.

"This was a mistake! The whole thing. You mark my words!" she yelled to the husband, who, in response, released into the toilet bowl a rattling, moist roar of flatulence that he'd been holding in since he'd first gone in and sat down.

HE'D SAVED HER. Her mother was certifiably deranged and her father was a known rapist. She remembers thinking on their first date, *At least I'll get my own house now.* It was years before she'd admit that to anyone, but there it was—she wanted her own place, with her own dishes and hand towels and family photos on the walls. He needed a new wife, and she was clean enough, polite enough, back then. He'd just gone up to her father in the yard one day and pointed, saying, "Could I take her on a date?" and her father said, "Sure you can. If you buy me a soda." So he came back the next evening in his truck with a six-pack of Pepsi. He took her out for milkshakes and a biscuit. The place they went to had giant biscuits. It was known for them.

The thing was, the blow dealt to him by the lesbian ex-wife was more than his stunted brain could endure, she decided, a year into the marriage. He was reasonably handsome and hard-working, but despite his noble posture and militant haircut, he turned out to be a broken-down stable horse with a burning-hot ego that would eventually incinerate him. It could only ever have been snuffed by the love of the lesbian who'd died a decade ago. How was the wife supposed to know this? It's not something you understand until it's too late. He'd caught the lesbian in bed with his own sister, more than once, engaged in a raunchy, possibly criminal position he'd not even known was possible. From what she could piece together of his cranky explanation, he'd beat his sister until her ears bled and begged the wife to denounce her same-sex attraction or else end up in a state hospital. Later he'd finally given up and said the ex-wife could do whatever she wanted so long as he occasionally watched from the broom closet, and if she promised never to divorce him. This contract was the tipping point, though, because the ex-wife left him shortly after and months later died in a car wreck. He insisted the crash was caused by one of her mentally unstable lovers. How could the ex-wife stand to be around him though, really, after he'd engaged in such groveling? It was doomed from the start, like so many things. The first wife was a beauty. The husband still kept a tooled leather album of their wedding photos in the lockbox. She never wore makeup and had the creamiest complexion, boyish, like potter's clay. She wore her black hair slicked back in a flip. Her breasts were magnificent, even under the high-necked oxfords she wore. He was a huge fan of magnificent breasts. The new wife kept hers on prominent display as well. Like she had a choice. It was a more liberal time and partially unbuttoned blouses were the thing the year they moved out of the city. He hated this constant presentation of her tits, unless they were alone. He was nothing if not possessive.

What was it that made denial turn into desire? the husband wondered to himself in private moments, smoking his cheap cigars on the wheel of the rusted-out combine, watching a gentle doe sneak behind the encircling birches.

When the children discovered they enjoyed the offal truck, the husband called them to be placed on the hydraulic lift at the rear, allowing them to ride up among the rancid waste barrels to watch the driver dump gallons of blood and sloppy innards into a maggot-infested trough. They held their noses and stared deeply into the thick pool of organs. The wife took great delight in explaining how the offal would be transformed into ladies' cosmetics at a nearby factory.

ONCE THINGS TOOK off, which didn't take long on account of the wife's ingratiating social skills, the previous owners appeared again, creeping slowly up the long drive in their flesh-colored Town Car. It was newly washed, the trim and wheels flashing in the sun. They lingered inexplicably within the vehicle, as if organizing something, before emerging from the hot car to stand with their hands in their pockets. Were they shy, or just old? The wife was incensed over not being allowed to make their acquaintance prior to the purchase. One look at those two, and she'd have advised him not to buy. She knew he knew this. She was a quick study in deceit. But what did they want? Nothing was certain about the two—every mannerly gesture seemed to conceal a filthier, feral motive. They meandered up to the office, waving as they walked through the door, as if the wife was expecting them and a graciousness ought to be extended for their having arrived on time for the appointment they never made.

They offered endless advice, in their eerie, matching voices. They delivered too-detailed histories of the facilities and the adjacent properties. "And of course this area was home to slaves. The help was necessary, and always humane. Now the neighboring estate is owned by a group of dykes and sodomites. So be cautious! Protect your children!"

"You mentioned that already," the wife said. But she could feel her husband burning behind her. She wouldn't turn around to see his face, but she could feel the heat melting the flesh off his hard bones.

"It was a booming business for us, and we paid all of our employees a fair wage," the lady said.

"When is this church service?" the husband asked, his

demeanor suddenly turning bright enough to blind them. "We have no taste for lewd behavior," he said. "None!"

"ABSOLUTELY NOT," SHE said to him later. "It's a damn cult. And why wouldn't they pay their employees fairly? Like they deserve a prize for being good to people." The whole conversation seemed beyond reason to her.

"We need to keep the peace!" he yelled, scolding her in the way he did when he'd reached his mysterious brink. His eruptions came without warning. Rarely did she see one coming.

"You should hire me," she said sweetly, trying to change the subject. "As a paid employee. I keep saying this. I want to pay taxes, honey! Pay into Social Security."

"There's no need for that! We're the fucking owners!" he said, still inflamed.

This would turn out to be a miserable, violent point of contention later in their lives, after they'd gone broke and were old and separated and her primary source of income came from his meager disability benefits. She'd continue to mention it long after he'd entered the nursing home, and even then he couldn't bring himself to admit she'd been right. Of course, his memory was eaten up and licked clean. Retribution rarely produced the rewards one hoped for.

"Do they think they're supposed to train us?" she'd whisper to her husband when the couple was around but out of earshot. He swatted her away with a wide, sharp cleaver flecked with fat.

"And these machines never gave us a bit of trouble," the couple said, gesturing toward the meat grinders. "They must be rinsed properly of an evening, or else there's a greater risk of malfunction. And the smokehouse must be sanitized."

The wife thought she was going to tear her own eyes out. The couple's pulsating voices enraged her. It was as if the two spoke on some rare frequency that triggered an area in her brain that longed for fantastic acts of torture.

"Now we've told you when the services are, right?" the lady said at the end of these visits. "So all that's left is for you to come! Oh, our pastor is truly touched. A true man of God! There's no excuse for you and your husband to say no."

Except the wife could think of nothing but. Even after so many months.

"We're buried these days! Business has really taken off," she reminded them, and it had. People from five counties were bringing their cows and hogs to be slaughtered and processed, and everyone poured out the compliments, especially regarding the sausage, and the transparency of prices. Every animal that came through the door was made as tranquil as a forest before the kill, they reminded the customers, assuring the most tender product. They'd even begun administering electroshock treatments to the beef, further tenderizing the carcass, a process that captivated the wife—watching the dead animal's muscles contract and relax each time the machine was switched on.

"Well, we had it going pretty good ourselves, but in the end we decided being full-time Christians was more important. A lot goes on in a true house of God that people don't know about!"

"I bet," the wife said, reeling.

The problem was that too many of the less conservative customers had already confessed an unnamable distrust of the
couple. Was it their matching voices and coordinated clothes?
One thing was, people questioned if the animal they'd brought
in was the butchered animal they collected on the other end.
Also, people claimed, the weights seemed incorrect. Most of all,
it was the communal suspicion surrounding the church's decision to pull all of their children out of the local school to be
enrolled in a private program owned by the church.

"Thanks must be given. Come show your appreciation!" the
lady said to the wife.

"We should thank you for how well our business is doing?"
the wife responded.

"Oh, mercy no! Not us, in particular. Your heavenly father!
Praise God for the blessings he's allowed you. Come give thanks
to God almighty!"

Hers had been a hard life. She'd always had trouble under-
standing other people's faith. Praise or penance never seemed to
yield the same results as backbreaking labor, in her experience.
So she just said it, and that was the glimmering pinnacle: "As far
as I can tell, we're the ones in here twelve hours a day, working
our hands to the bone. So I'll just thank myself, if you don't
mind."

The lady backed up a few steps, opening her mouth wider
than the wife thought possible. The uvula was dark red and
swollen. "We have no intention of permitting an atheist to run
our business!" she finally managed to say, putting her hands up
in front of her, as if warding off an attack.

"Well, it's too late for that. It's already been sold to us. And I think you should leave."

That evening while the husband lay in bed sweating, boiling over her intolerance and the thought of the lesbians next door, his wife stood out in the yard beside the old water pump, breathing heavily under a sky busted apart with stars, smelling the rancid hay in the fields, gazing across the acres at a blurry spot along the fence where she was certain she saw someone standing, staring back at her in the dark. Perhaps there were two silhouettes, even, holding hands by the gravel road? Her housedress whipped around her legs in the breeze and her mind leaped forward many decades to a vision of her adult children sitting before her on an elegantly decorated sunporch, both of them making a depressed, pathetic case for why they wanted nothing to do with their father. "He never loved us unconditionally!" they exclaimed. "He didn't provide a nurturing environment!" They had unhealthy adult bodies, and malformed child-faces. This whole exchange would come to pass, subtracting the part about the sunporch and adding the latent disgust they eventually extended to her too, ducking her embrace whenever she reached for them, which was often. She'd remember this night in the yard and her vague premonition of the children delivering back to their father the selfish negligence he'd sowed into their child-hearts. This accordion of memories would leave her feeling fated and alive and connected to every detail—the sharpening rod on the stoop, the red chiggers swarming on the well, the bark peeling off the birches, the crowded nettles. Of the moment in the country when everything fell apart. The endless growl from the electric engine of an oil horse in the field behind the sodomites' ranch style brought her back. She went inside and slipped under the sheets next to her husband, who was playing over in his pre-sleep the inevitable argument he'd have with his wife when he finally told her he was, in fact, only leasing the slaughterhouse, and the option to buy was contingent on a list of indecipherable stipulations that he'd hardly even read, having been so eager to escape the city and begin the messy, glorious business of killing animals on a farm.

Perhaps he was an idiot after all.

"Are we supposed to be polite to them now?" she asked him. He hadn't said a word to her all day. This wasn't uncommon. They were leaning over the stainless industrial sink, scrubbing dried blood from under their fingernails. "They don't even strike me as the type to get their hands dirty!" she said. "How did they ever manage a slaughterhouse?"

"How do you think? They had mutual respect! They honored each other," he said, looking at his bloody apron.

As it turned out, they were indeed the type to get their hands dirty. Or at least the type to pay someone else to get their hands dirty for them. Filthy, actually, because the husband and wife returned from a cattle auction a week later to find the entire killing floor flooded with sewage. The septic tank had backed up and seeped beneath the locker room door, filling the place with the smell of shit, ruining all the uncured meat. They had to pay back the price of all the hogs and cattle that were contaminated.

"We're in deep now!" the husband said, throwing his rubber gloves at her, going for the phone. "You're going to call and fix this. You're going to that church."

"You want me to pray over a backed-up septic tank? When did you turn so pious?" She could see the bile spilling over his face in response to her having used a word he didn't know. "Religious!" she said. "For God sakes."

"The moment those two walked into our house and invited us to church. Now you're going to call them, ask for the name of their plumber, tell them you're a stupid person and we'll see them at the next service."

"What have you done?" she said coldly. "What do we owe? What kind of dirty deal did you strike?"

"We'll lose this place!" he screamed, spit flying from his mouth, his eyes going bloodshot.

"Good riddance," she said, wading out of the putrid waste, using the mop to clear a slimy path before her.

HE TRIED TO make amends with the couple. She could hear them both on the other end of the phone when he called, speaking sedately in their twin voices, saying how sorry they were to hear of the sad trouble that had befallen the business. "Satan is a cunning thief," they said. "Have you considered that the disturbed neighbors are possibly to blame? Those deviants?" they asked.

He had considered that. "It's a little closer to home though," the husband said after hanging up, eyeing his wife with teeth-grinding contempt.

"It's them you should be angry at, you old fool! Or yourself. Not me!"

"It's Satan, all right," he said to her. "Lucifer herself!" He pitched a jar of meat jelly at her from the kitchen doorway. It went sailing past, crashing against the wall, where it dripped sluggishly down the floral paper.

The next week the water heater exploded, damaging the entire south end of the house. A few days after that, the propane tank acquired a leak, leaving them without gas to cook a meal. For the final, exhausting toll, a health inspector showed up to do a full review of the facilities, announcing a list that included over ten thousand dollars' worth of necessary renovations in order for them to remain in operation. They had five days to comply, or else close the doors. "God bless," the inspector said, as he bowed his head beside the lard vat.

Later that day, as he wrapped up the last hog's leg, the husband whispered to her, tenderly almost, "You've cursed us."

The first moment she had to herself, she snuck up into the attic alone to embroider in a broken easy chair. The hypnotic rhythm of precise work allowed her to slide below her own imagination, the whole history of the world, even, to a place where a woman didn't need a husband. The peaceful, slippery dream didn't last long. It was nearly visible though. Was it his disgust she feared? Sure, his blood curdled at the thought of taking advice from her. He couldn't help that. It was purely physical. But when she finally tried to explain, on the ride home from their lawyer's office, he turned and spit on her. "Oops," he said as they stared at the gooey clots of chewing tobacco on her legs and shoes.

"I put flour under all of the doormats at night and every time we left the house," she said. "And every time when we came back I lifted the mats to find footprints in the flour. They've been coming in our house and the business since we moved here."

He hated her for being clever, more than anything.

AND AS IT turned out the old lockbox had a gun in it. Why didn't she know about that? After the children had gone to sleep, he sat beside her in bed holding the pistol, running the tip of it up her arm, and then her cheek. The air conditioner had just quit working and the heat was so thick they were floating in it. He said, "You stupid, ugly woman. I could kill you right now." She peed herself, and blinked as a tear rolled down her huge nose. He gave a dumb, satisfied smile, showing bits of tobacco in his brown teeth. She could smell the hay and trees outside the open bedroom window, mixed with his body odor, which, like always, was a fermented, yeasty smell because of all the bread he ate. His doctor had asked more than once how much he drank, because of the smell. He didn't drink at all, she'd said. He was merely intoxicated with buried fury and yeast.

She looked over at him, pointed a shaky finger at his bare, concave chest. "You do it now then," she said, "because if you don't kill me I'll make you wish you had from now until forever."

Of course he didn't do it. He was never going to. He just wanted to see the look on her face when he produced the secret, black gun and held it to her head. Would she pray then?

Not at all.

She did make him regret it though. Always and forever.

All of the gossipy women in town reached out to her when the business closed and her husband went back to the city, leaving her and the children alone in the country while he got things settled, again. The past in reverse, again. How was it that she was the one who remained, stranded in her husband's rural dream? The women came by smiling, bringing dense foods to console her. One in particular—the widowed prison guard with spiky red hair, standing so tall she had to look down at nearly everyone—ordered the wife to stay with her after the official eviction date.

When the husband finally called for her this time, the wife said no thank you.

She grew to love the prison guard dearly, and the prison guard loved her, though not in any sexual way, unfortunately. The wife let the husband think what she knew he would until his memory was consumed. He'd already decided that any woman not obviously flattered by his attention was a homosexual. The world, it turned out, was full of rude lesbians, insisting they open their own car door and carry their own groceries, insulted by an honest compliment from an assertive man. The wife had discovered the kind of retribution that would keep on giving without her having to do much at all, the kind he could enact all on his own, in the privacy of his boring nights as he roamed aimlessly around his cluttered apartment, listening to the distressing noise of cars and gunshots and neighbors yelling, in that city he used to know so well but no longer understood, being too old and entitled to comprehend the longing or poverty or bound-up rage of anyone more complicated than himself.

When the wife began to bleed occasionally from her nose and eyes, her friend made her nettle tea. The old doctor at the clinic appeared nervous before the lab results, eventually referring her to the doctor in the city. Her friend came in with a paper bag full of nettle leaves she'd picked in an abandoned lot across the street. She dumped them carefully into a pot of boiling water on the stove. It made the house smell like dead plants. She strained the leaves from the golden water through a metal sieve into a mason jar. They drank it together on the sofa while watching *Matlock*. It was hard to tell if it did any good, but it tasted nice, like rain and rot, and it made the wife feel content.

When she saw the Christian lady again, many years later, they were in the Dollar General store. The wife and her friend were cackling at each other, trying on stupid hats in front of a small, warped mirror affixed to the sunglasses kiosk. The lady appeared like a distortion between their grinning reflections. She was reaching for an item she could hardly grasp on a high shelf. The wife turned around, as if searching out something, to watch the lady feebly lifting a giant can into her cart. She had aged tremendously, her wide back hunched and her hair so thin the scalp was shining beneath the harsh lights of the store. The wife had read in the newspaper last winter how the man had fallen over in the driveway at night and froze to death, and of course she'd read about the church scandal. It wasn't exactly satisfaction she felt. She had to admit there were things she'd never considered about the couple:

1. That they hadn't wanted to sell the business in the first place. That the church had forced them. Everyone in the congregation had liquidated their personal assets in preparation for an apocalypse. The pastor had charged himself with the obligation of constructing an underground haven where they could all await the Second Coming. No haven was ever constructed. The money disappeared and the pastor was in prison. It was not long after that the sexual abuse allegations came out, regarding the children attending the private school.

2. The couple didn't know how to trust anyone. How could they? They'd worked their whole lives for something and lost it. Being lied to had made them liars too.

She couldn't stop herself from following the lady out into the parking lot, where she labored again with a case of canned food beside her car. The wife approached softly. "Let me help you with that, please," she said. The lady didn't look up. She stayed fixed on the difficult task.

"No thank you," she said blankly, without any sign of recognition.

The wife reached out. "That's too bad, because I've already decided I'm going to help you," she said, taking the heavy load.

The Book-Eating Ceremony

Rage loiters in me, like those welfare mothers always on the Internet at the public library. Dating sites is what they're doing. My rage is similar: ignorant and sexual. I have degrees, sure. Though I will say, none of them are in frames—such a tacky, insecure ethos. Recently, as an excuse to leave town for a few days, I attended the Women's Cultural Studies Convention in Grand Rapids. Immediately I was depressed. The hotel decor was too menacing, the wallpaper a tableau of shaggy oxen flanked by rosebuds resembling human livers. The women used too many words, were all fetishists of their own bad ideas, constantly scribbling in the margins of everything: New books, obscure journals, takeout menus. "Marginalia," they liked to say. "Your marginalia is extensive!" or "Pardon me, I wasn't trying to peek at your marginalia!" Like scientists in a singles bar. The self-satisfied jargon. The pretend poetry.

Shit and fall back in it. Just give me the goddamned discourse.

The keynote speaker was an astounding bitch. Premier

pornography scholar and behavioral theorist Trisha Gregory. I couldn't take my eyes off her. She had a runty, rat face. Her hair was a tangle of frizzed chestnut with a patch of white that fell over one eye, like she was an erotic villain. During her address she pointed at people, delivered degrading analyses of everyone's body language. The topic was "Performative Proximity." I'd never heard of it either. The audience squirmed and giggled, until it was their turn. Several walked out of the old red hall with their arms gruffly crossed, prompting Trisha to serenely whisper into her little microphone, "Take note of the closed posturing as the offended exit the room. One might assume they're asserting a dominant stance, but this configuration only serves to further demonstrate the rawness of their vulnerability." The microphone was very close to her mouth. The words hissed through the hall like a mechanical snake.

Afterward, in the lounge, I drank too much. Trisha was there, reveling in her own disdain, surrounded by a gaggle of elderly lesbians. I wedged between them to order more wine. "Audacious presentation!" I said, not meaning to sound so enthusiastic. She smoked a long, black cigarette and stared at a painting on the wall of a woman wearing a dress made of parrots. I reached out to shake her hand. I mentioned my own research. It came out strewn and incompetent. I continued to blabber until I'd finished my merlot. She seemed exceptionally slim, right up to the hips, where she carried an alarming width that narrowed abruptly again after the knees. She said she needed to use the restroom. Something about the tone, the raise of her immense eyebrow, suggested I follow her. We went to her hotel room, where she offered me more wine and asked if I was into fisting.

"I thought you had to use the restroom?" I said.

She stared at me.

"I don't know. I've never done it," I said. I stood unsteadily before the tinted hotel window, feeling insane in my cheap slacks. Moments later I found myself being finger-banged on the bed while being called the most terrible names. I did not call her names, but slept on the floor afterward using my ugly pants as a pillow.

In the morning she offered me a copy of her most recent book, *Morphologies: The Undoing of Eden*. I asked her to sign it. She already had a pen out, flicked her name in a giant loop across the final page. "You should include a number," I said, "where you might be reached."

Her pen hovered in a bored, reluctant way, but she obliged. "Don't ever call me," she said, in a sad tone.

MY PARTNER, MIRIAM, is dying. Primary peritoneal carcinoma. She's resigned herself to it and stopped treatment over a year ago, before we even met. Two months into the relationship she decided to reveal this. She didn't expect us to last so long, she said. Miriam was a new lesbian. Her illness offends me. Of Trisha, Miriam would probably say I'm being destructive. Death ripens the heart, turns it soft and penetrable as rotten fruit. I suppose I want that same: the freedom to destroy myself in whatever manner I see fit.

Back in Kentucky, I drive directly from the airport to the

university. I drink purified water in the Women's Studies Department where I currently hold the position of the Belva P. Fanny Chair in Sexuality. This is not a title I like to say aloud, for obvious reasons. The office is too dim. The tiny lights of the office equipment blink with tired alarm. I am on sabbatical, and it's a Saturday, so I won't have to encounter any chatty colleagues or dumb-eyed, homely students. I clip things from old medical journals. I xerox photographs of vulvas. Vaginas are such varied items. One, a hillside of wheat split by a narrow path. Another, a window gaping out into nothing—some lonely warmer dimension. Others, if you squint, are like gutted rock quarries. At home, I will tack the pages up like wallpaper in the dining room, a collage to the pioneers of modern gynecology. But also, a crime scene, a repository of clinical smut, a pervert's dossier! This is not the living situation of an adult. But I am writing a book. Working title: The Dyke Pageant. It is an investigation, among other things, into the failures of Albert H. Decker, M.D., D.O.G. He is the source, in my opinion, of decades of misinformation. I was more fervent when I first began. A year has passed. Things are different. I am still waiting for a viable theory to discover itself—something beyond "This guy was an idiot and asshole." I long to lurch like a mad person from the sludge pit of academia, if one can even use the word "academia" in the same sentence as Eastern Kentucky University. But I am interested in paychecks, unlimited access to the copy machine.

ANOTHER THING: MY mother died two winters ago, and I'm living in her house—a rural outpost on three acres of the

Daniel Boone National Forest. On the drive home I listen to the university library's only available audio recording of Trisha Gregory. It is her first book, *Substrata of Outsider Erotica*, read by the author. I pay more attention to her voice than to the theories. Her tone is even more dramatic on tape, like an oboe filled with gravel.

Outside of Bowling Green the bald landscape undoes itself, rising into the foothills of the Appalachians. A heavy rain tears ditches along the side of the highway. The house is outside of Williamsburg, off the road, concealed among a row of crooked hemlocks. I turn down the drive just as the last sight of light drains off behind the pines.

Miriam and her dogs are asleep in the spare room, tangled up like dirty rags on the bed. Miriam is an animal lover. Which might explain why she's with me. She saves the mangiest strays. Last week, she nabbed a lab from the parking lot at Auto Zone. Being a kind of scientist, I find great sadness in the domestication of animals. She stays in the spare room with the mutts most nights, claiming I grind my teeth during sleep. I retire late and wake before her. She sleeps often. I write and read and take long walks in the woods. Sometimes she'll get up and ask to come with me. Sometimes I let her. On the walks she asks about Mother: the time she found a finger floating in a can of green beans, details of her rural girlhood and, Miriam's favorite, the one about Mother hearing voices in the neighbor's barn. Miriam's interest in Mother annoys me. With Miriam here, I dream of Mother too often and with an eerie lucidity.

I like the house. I feel something for it, in the way one might feel toward another human, but with less contempt. It was Mother's childhood home, where she returned to live and die after her second divorce. It was always a disintegrating place. Her father built the original cabin in 1931. I remember, as a girl, pulling back a loose corner of carpet to see the year carved into a floorboard. The place was once a one-room cabin in the woods but is now an expansive maze of poorly built additions with a crumbling chimney jutting out like a lumpy phallus.

DEAD ANIMALS ROT in the undergrowth and plants rise up in purples and yellows like colorful claws reaching from the corpses. Algae grows on everything. Lichen suture themselves to rocks and feather out in crooked strands. Decay swells in every direction—like a concerto, or a rash.

Eastern Kentucky is the Half-South. They say "worsh" instead of "wash." "Yonder" instead of "over there." There is something sinister in the clangor of the dialect.

These are not my people. I run from them. I turn away in public places.

When I received the call saying Mother was dead, I honestly wanted to feel something. But I was just thirsty. I was sleeping, alone in my bed. I pictured her alone too, sitting in the recliner in the cabin, eating fruit from a can. She had not lived here for many years. It had sat empty, with her in Shepherds Manor. I imagined wild animals had moved in, were breeding and nesting in the bedrooms, pissing on the furniture. I pictured saplings jimmying apart the floorboards. When I did move in, months later, the place was like a water-damaged issue of *Antique Living*. There were stacks of broken-down cereal boxes and Banquet dinner trays piled like turrets on either side of the stove. A raccoon crawled out of the fireplace.

It is still saturated with odors, suspended in Mother's weary attempt to have it seem middle-class. It groans occasionally with an old woman's desire to return to the dirt and trees.

I settle into the paraphernalia. The thesis of Trisha's book, as far as I can tell: "The physical body is a reflection of internal desire. It communicates all emotions through inadvertent gesticulations." Is this news? She claims that when we are deliberately projecting one emotion, a truer, more private one is exposed, uncontrollably. Albert Decker would agree with this, except he'd call these symptoms of "a delinquent behavioral process." "Bisexualism in females," according to *Decker's Office Gynecology*, is "characterized by variations toward a masculine constitution: great height, broad and bony shoulders, a narrow and only slightly inclined pelvis; her thighs will not touch, she will possess outstanding artistic talent, above-average intelligence." Nowhere does he mention absolute lesbianism, the insipid or ignorant butch—only a clever, perverted housewife.

THE REFRIGERATOR IS full of salad dressings and there is a sad assortment of empty potato chip bags tucked beneath the sofa cushions. Miriam did the grocery shopping again. She is hungry always for these nonfoods. I sneak out onto the deck and phone Trisha but hang up after three rings.

Miriam hunches like a dope before the dog bowl, scraping bacon off her plate. The idiot mutts nip at each other's faces.

I am a particular woman. I have developed a romance with the arrangement of data. All photos and specimens are defined and annotated in the exhaustive legend I keep in corresponding notebooks: the uterine sound, the Pederson speculum, the cervical cannula. Sometimes, in the early hours, while looking at the photos, I am struck by a lustful gruesomeness. Decker too was a fussy record keeper, with an aversion to surgical gloves, one will notice, as he holds back the labia in his patients' photo logs. Even as I wallow in his errors, I respect the tenacity. In the X-rays over his light box the stern bones of the dyke glowed like fluorescent cylinders. He could point as easy as if it were on an atlas, to the specific location of her psychic imbalance, her emotional conflict and sterility. His was the premier science of justified homophobia.

Miriam insists I see the hummingbird feeders she's hung from the branches of the gingko tree, like a Christmas tree for hummingbirds. There is an infestation. I stand next to the tree in a red baseball cap and the birds rush my head. I keep still. Miriam whispers, "Don't open your mouth, Adelaide. They'll fly right in." She hoots, swats one away with her plump hand. She asks if people can eat hummingbird. "Of course," I say, "in some countries they eat live hummingbirds, snatch them out of the air mid-flight and bite directly into the breast. Certain quick-reflex, small-handed women and gay men are especially good at snatching the birds."

"Really?" she asks.

"You're a goon," I say.

The dogs line up on the other side of the sliding glass door, begging to get out. Miriam is laughing as she slides it back. The bastards charge. The sound of the barking and Miriam's laughter causes the birds to scatter. They race like a squadron out of the yard and over the frog pond. They're very nervous animals. "Bitches! Fuckers!" I yell at them.

After dinner Miriam plays her Eagles CD on the stereo and opens all the windows so that a grass-filled breeze blows through the house. I help her up onto the giant oak dining table. She slides out of her culottes, lays her face on the table and shows me her ass. She keeps her knees tight against her chest. Her backside is like a monstrous, pink beach ball, her thighs goose-pimpled. I press my mouth against the hood, my chin to the opening. I close my eyes and suck her clitoris. I lubricate my hands with oil. And fold them. I insert two fingers, then four. I keep the fingertips together as I penetrate her. It's like turning down the slickest cul-de-sac. While giving her head I think of a CPR class I took in college, of the plastic doll used to demonstrate mouth-to-mouth. Her vagina has that plastic taste, except more tart, like spring water.

"What was that about?" she asks later, eating shredded cheese folded in a pickle slice. Toy tacos, she calls them.

"Did it hurt?" I ask.

"Was that the point?"

"No."

"Well, it felt good. When I'm with you I feel better for some reason," she says.

"I feel unruly," I say.

ON THE ROTTEN deck I read. I call Trisha again but she does not pick up.

I force myself to work. I sit down and draft an outline of chapter three, which, as of today, I'm calling "The Cunt Curator." I end up making a long list of alternative chapter titles: "Twat Collector," "Homeward Bound 4: The Reckoning," "Toy Tacos."

Decker reads the body like a textbook. "Masculine traits," he writes, "in the modern female, are quite often evidence of a physiological and psychological disorder." In his photo logs, which I scrutinize too often, the labia part and the vaginal openings distend, as if to venerate their own meticulous architecture. In my outline I write: "Science is a scrupulous attack of the self. Show me an unhealthy craving and I'll show you a pocket-knife."

I have no idea what this means. A hummingbird has gotten into the house and snapped its neck during an effort at escaping through the skylight. I sweep it off the floor into the dustpan; it lands in the trash with a tender thud. Minutes later the dogs have toppled the can and are fighting over the soggy corpse.

WHEN I FIRST met Miriam she was standing beside a truck loaded with yard ornaments, wearing a hot-pink tracksuit, holding a greasy paper sack in front of Big Dog's barbecue stand. She was crying, in an obvious way. I walked past her with my head down, to order my loose meat sandwich. I could hear her talking to herself while I watched a ragged teen spoon coleslaw into a Styrofoam cup. On the way back to my car she yelled, "Hey!

Hey, girl! Hold up. Listen." She'd locked her keys in the cab. She was still wiping tears off her face when she asked if I'd give her a ride. And there was her neck, like a short loaf of bread, and her forehead, flat as a tabletop.

She is not a beautiful woman. She is malleable, capable of filling small rooms with her body. I imagine hiding things in her heft. Her voice is shrill as a kazoo.

Now we're lesbians of the land: twin valves opening against each other in the darkness of the master bedroom, contrary figures hoeing rows in the garden. We are the cat and the crawfish. Other times, the lady and the friend. I hold the dogs back while she cleans their pen.

THE LIBRARIAN'S FINGERS seem swollen. I detect a smell of Lysol as he hands me my ordered books. I read at a little desk made for a child and watch the man climb a stepladder in order to reshelve the reference material. The welfare mothers peck ferociously at their keyboards while their dirt-faced children wander among the stacks. In her third book, *Meta Porn Heroine*, Trisha writes: "A researcher will often find herself blocked by the biases of her own deductions, even as an object's meaning mutates before her. One is handicapped, as in life, by the malfunctions of our own prejudices and desires. It should come as no surprise that these personal preoccupations are rampant among leading pornographic scholars." I want to discuss this with the little librarian. Instead I gather my things. I could apply Trisha's logic to a mailbox if I thought long enough about it. Every idea lands sharply, and then ripples into nothing. At home

I call her again. This time someone answers, a man. He says his name is Landon and he's feeding the fish. "Trisha is in Bucharest," he says.

"For how long?" I ask.

He claims to take down a message but when I ask him to repeat my number back he says, "I'm off. Thank you!"

The call throws me into a panic for the rest of the day.

There are four photos of patient D568 in Decker's source material, with either her eyes blocked out or the face softly blurred. Her body, though, is always unmistakable and vulgar. At forty-two years old, D568 is as awkward and angular as an adolescent male. Decker charted the patient's development over thirty years, like a timeline for biological deviance. "Prototypical housewife-queer" he calls her. She looks like me. We're of the same "sexless" frame. There is a blank utility about her, suggesting only shapes. I feel less lonely when I look at her.

I take out a sheet of paper and write across the top, "I am my own test subject."

MIRIAM AND I go to a bar. My hair is clean and I'm wearing a button-down shirt. What is here for the irreverent dyke? Pole barns, a sad library, Walmart, endless isolated hollers full of coyotes. Miriam is sitting with her girlfriends and wearing a dress she made herself from a checkered tablecloth. There is a hole cut in it for her head. I buy drinks for everyone. "Doesn't she put you in the mood for a picnic?" I ask her friends. She laughs but her friends hurry toward the dartboard. They seem defensive in their leather skirts and tight T-shirts. Each of their shirts has something printed on it: DRAMA QUEEN, ROCK STAR, DIVA. They are all over forty. "Are those their Christian names?" I ask Miriam.

"No," she says. "Those are job descriptions."

She shotguns several beers and we attempt a clumsy game of pool. She insists we leave and go for barbecue. We drive and eat the sandwiches. Miriam makes a mess of herself. She is a tablecloth smeared with barbecue sauce. She wants to show me a field. "I've seen one before," I say. We arrive and we get out of the car and she points to some lines cut into the tall grass. "I don't get it," I say.

"Look at it for a minute," she says.

So I do. I stare for a long time until suddenly I can see that there are words mowed into the wheat. You have to tilt your head a bit, lean against the grass. "Hello," it says, and then just a few yards away, "Goodbye."

"Ain't that something? Drama Queen's husband did it with a riding mower."

"Looks time-consuming," I say. Miriam turns to cough. She hacks for a minute and out of nowhere vomits onto the ground. She heaves a few more times, until it seems there's nothing left. I consider putting my hand on her back but she vomits so casually it seems silly to comfort her. It just falls right out of her mouth. She has the simplest expression on her face. She has done this many times. Her thin hair twirls around her head in the wind. When she has finally finished she says, "I'm sorry I threw up." She pulls up her dress to wipe off her mouth. I get a full shot of her legs, sturdy and pale and vast. "Do you mind if we go home? I smell like puke," she says.

Half-asleep on the sofa, with Miriam in the spare room, I touch myself. I think of her legs and Trisha's head, of the place where Miriam's thighs begin to touch right above the knee, her enormous backside, the outline so visible through the thin fabric of that terrible dress. I think of the abrupt transition between Trisha's waist and her unbelievable hips, her clever insults. I climax to the image of their ghastly hybrid.

I HAVE CLIPPED Trisha's photo from the dust jacket of *Morphologies and Eden* and taped it inside my desk drawer, next to the unsharpened pencils. I open the drawer too often. "Let your life be a document for the world to study and despise!" the prologue reads. Her words are a confirmation, of something: every pervert distinguishes herself by the manner in which she chooses to condemn others?

Typically, in the earlier stages of theoretical discourse, pages amass until a puzzle appears. I'm supposing here. I've never written a book before. I have an inkling and a self-imposed deadline. There is repetition, I know that, and hypotheses extending like slippery tentacles. There are paragraphs lined up like the variables of a long equation with no solution. Drowning comes to mind, a constant sense of doom. In this way you can tell a book is alive.

I dream of Mother. I am looking out the kitchen window. She is outside, holding a bucket. She is looking cautiously into the bucket, as if it contains something dangerous. I open the kitchen window.

"The neighbor!" she yells sulkily. "He and I want you to have this!"

"What's this regarding?" I ask, pretending not to recognize her.

"This here's birdseed." She smiles like a crook. She is proud of the birdseed, I realize. "The neighbor used to make it for me all the time. I was a good woman, Adelaide. You might wanna fill them feeders since I can't do it." She nods in the direction of the numerous bird feeders that hang from the awnings.

"No," I say. "You're dead."

"I know," she says, sitting the bucket down. "Have your friend fill them anyway."

She turns around to face the rigid pines, where the creek splits the woods. She removes her old blue bandana and scratches her head. "See you later," she says. Her gait seems angry, but she gives me a little wave as she crosses the bridge.

"Thank you," I whisper.

MASSES OF PAPERWORK, big boxes of manila folders stuffed with menacing, shadowy xeroxes. Books stacked waist-high around the desk. So many naked women and illustrations of arcane gynecological equipment, orifices packed tight with instruments, X-rays of fallopian tubes shimmering with dye.

"Maybe I'm a masochist?" I say to Miriam over lunch.

"Are those the people who eat their own hair and fingernails?" she asks.

I offer her more cooked carrots.

"My friends used to call me the Nursing Home," she says.

"Why?" I ask.

"I was the place where all the old men went to die." She laughs enormously, making a spectacle of herself, showing her fat tongue, pink as chewed-up gum.

"All of your boyfriends were senior citizens?" I ask. She likes to make me guess at things.

"More or less," she says. "I feel my weight has kept me from finding a good husband."

I can't tell if she's joking this time. I'm inclined to say it has more to do with her face, but I don't. "There's someone for everyone," I say. "You should move to a big city."

"No," she says. "That's not an option. Maybe there are other options here now," she says, piling carrots onto a slice of buttered bread.

"Doubtful," I say.

AFTER LUNCH WE follow the little creek through the trees.

"I even dated Rupert," she says, "the old dude who lived over yonder. We once were engaged. He's passed now. It was intense though," she says. "Which is why it didn't last. He was too demanding, sexually."

"I can't imagine," I say, though I can. This was Mother's old neighbor. I'm forced to picture Rupert and Miriam together. His feeble gnome body perched on top of Miriam's beastly thighs, stabbing into the folds.

"And I'm only thirty-nine," she says, smiling, shyly fluffing her hair with her palm, as if to signal she knows she looks good for age. She indeed has the face of a giant infant. "You know how people can be," she says. "They want a woman to be their everything and then nothing at all."

We cross the bridge. We walk through the woods until we hit the tree line. There is a long stretch of electric fence. The grass is sparse and I can see ragged animals bending to graze at scattered blotches of green.

"He loved his goats," Miriam says. "His daughter takes care of them now."

"He's the one," I say, "that Mother used to work for when she was a teenager. The one that grew dry corn. And my Mother would shell it."

"Oh!" Miriam says. "For feed. He *loves* feeding things," she says, winking, running her hands over her solid, head-sized breasts. She makes a loud clicking noise with her tongue and the goats lift their heads. A few of them amble over, but change their minds and eat more grass instead. "Do you feel closer to your Mother here?" she asks.

"I don't think so," I say.

"I do," she says.

The story Miriam always wants to hear is one Mother used to tell me when I was a kid, about the shelling of corn for Rupert. Mother described the hand-cranked sheller he kept in the barn, and how hard she had to work to get the corn through. She was working in the barn after school one day when a man whispered to her from outside the barn. "Lucille, when will you come for me?" he said. My mother's face always scared me when she described the voice. Her eye would twitch. Like someone had called up to her from the hottest caverns of hell. It was one of those dizzying childhood moments when I knew she wasn't just my mother but also a woman living alone in the world. She'd asked what the man meant and when he didn't answer she stepped out of the barn to see that no one was there, just the goats chewing garlic near the fence.

I AM FEELING troubled today by how similar my build is to patient D568. Perhaps my arms are longer, my shoulders narrower? The whole endeavor is beginning to feel like fodder. I play the game again where I allow my eyes to fall out of focus so that the vaginas are not vaginas but instead: sea slugs; aquatic plant life; dry, veiny leaves; compact mounds of fresh clay. I'm waiting to stumble upon a formula. I wouldn't consider myself the sort of person who sees patterns where there are none, though maybe I am not myself. It seems important to acknowledge how consistently we are encouraged to see ourselves in such uniform ways, goaded into it, slowly, from girlhood to old age, enticed by the shallow rewards that come with correctly performing our femininity. Like a hot, horny pork chop dangling from a string, a diamond ring on a razor-sharp fish hook. And we are marginalized, of course, if we can't produce femininity in a recognizable way. One becomes prone to imagining her body in a dozen untrue ways. Every mirror is a funhouse mirror.

MIRIAM RETURNS FROM the grocery store with all the dogs in the back of her pickup truck. She's wearing the same clothes she had on yesterday. Her hair looks uncombed, the curls tangled and jutting out in odd directions. The dark circles under her eyes have grown more pronounced. She snaps the truck door closed with her powerful hip. "Trudy! Timmy," she yells, prompting the dogs to leap out of the truck. The two small ones trail behind. The other two chase each other around the yard like manic children. Their names are, shamefully, Pat and Benatar. "I'd have ten more if I could afford to feed them!" she says, always, to anyone who shows the slightest interest. They make my skin crawl, most days, especially when Miriam wants to discuss what will happen to them when she dies. All day the dogs are in tow, their claws clicking like tap shoes on the hardwood. The deception of dogs disgusts me. The lie of pretending to lead, when of course they're just following in front, looking back constantly for approval. I ask Miriam if she'd like to help me plant the garden. She says, "I would! How wonderful," clapping her hands together, exciting the dogs. When I look at her, when I see her reaching to pick up the terrier, or straining to pull the detergent from the shelf above the washing machine, I imagine pulling off her khakis and pressing my mouth against her anus. I want to own her, and please her.

AT THE FEED store a gathering urge overwhelms me. I fill my basket to the brim with seeds. Miriam has rented a gas-powered tiller. It turns out to be a joyously loud machine that is often hard to handle but fun because it is so unwieldy and tough. After the ground is ready we consult one of Mother's books to determine the best method of planting. On one end is a variety of greens, the other tubers and corms. When you're standing on the hill near the shed, the fresh plot looks like a grid. The parallel lines are comforting. The dogs trot the perimeters. They wrestle like mongoloids in the grass. After dinner I find my favorite hairbrush half-chewed under the buffet in the hall.

Miriam goes into town for dinner and the moment she's out of the house I phone Trisha. I leave a message this time, telling her that she should come for a visit. I water the garden and read in a lawn chair near the woods. When I go back into the house there is a message on the machine. I am sweating as I play it back. Trisha's voice is tired and cold. She declines the invitation, saying her schedule is full. She sighs into the receiver and quotes Foucault: "We return to those empty spaces, don't we, Adelaide, that have been masked by omission or concealed in a false or misleading plentitude?"

I return her call but she does not pick up. I leave a message as well. "When I think of Foucault," I say, nearly screeching, "I can't help but imagine a bridge troll in a bobby helmet with an ass full of anal beads. So it's hard to take what you're saying seriously." I sit by the phone for almost half an hour before giving up and dialing Miriam's cell instead.

"When are you coming back?" I ask.

"Never," she says. "Or in a couple of hours."

ANOTHER DREAM OF Mother: "I'll get you a shovel," she yells from the bridge, her boots booming on the planks, a tear in the seat of her overalls so big you can see her long johns. She heads in the direction of the goats. Miriam has her head stuck out of the kitchen window, giving me a stupid look.

I say, "What are you doing, eavesdropping?"

She says, "I can hear you talking to your mother even if you think I can't. Don't do this, Adelaide."

"Don't do what?" I say, lying, because I know I'm working out a deal of some kind with Mother. "You'll thank me later," I tell Miriam. "Get the animals ready!" Miriam slams the window down without taking the prop off the sill. The rod splinters everywhere. Mother comes back with a shovel.

"You're going to need this," she says.

When I open my eyes there is the stiff, ridiculous sense of an omen on me. I hate the feeling.

I SIT ON a bucket and leaf through *Nonoperative Physical Measures in Gynecology*. It's probably not something a person should get worked up over, but I do. They've got these women spread wider than the Cumberland Gap, most of the faces carefully cut out, an alluring anonymity that stirs my libido like a spoon.

I stay out late, making notes in the back of my book and watching the sun do its little show along the property line before it burns off completely into the woods. Inside I rinse sweet potatoes. I ask Miriam to cook them for dinner. She is bitching about another headache, more nausea. She says she needs brown sugar to make the potatoes but we don't have any. "Sweet potatoes is made with brown sugar not white," she says.

I say, "Get off your ass and go get some." She bends down to scratch Trudy. She rubs the dog behind the ears before walking off down the hallway where she figures I can't see her. She stands there a long time just staring down at the carpet. After a while she comes back into the room and plucks the keys from the hook. "I'm going to the store to get the brown sugar," she says. "Will you ever finish this book?"

"I doubt it," I say.

"What else do we need?"

"A bag of ideas. A pound of insight," I say.

"Vanishing now," she says. "Poof. Goodbye."

IF I GET at Miriam slow enough and long enough I can bury my hand inside of her. Once it's in, I open my fist slow and lissome as a cloud. It is then that she is my property.

Lately the dogs spend too much time inside the house. I chase them into their pens with a flyswatter and in an hour Miriam has let them out again. As soon as she unlatches the doors they run about and abuse the furniture. How quickly an outdoor dog becomes an indoor pet. Fuck you, Miriam. I never wanted dogs. She lugs them around like infants. How willing those dogs are to please, to soil the rug, to return later to a shit stain and lap at the ghost of their own waste.

MIRIAM AND I stand near the toolshed. "The hysterectomy was wrong," she says. She's emotional today.

"Mother had one," I say. "Like removing perishables from a broken-down refrigerator!"

"Children were just always something I thought I might like," she says.

"Just thinking about little children makes me want to drink," I say. "This is why you treat those damn dogs like babies," I say.

"In a way, I'm sure," she says.

She weaves a small wreath out of weeds—black medic, some wood sorrel. She presents it to me. It fits perfectly around my wrist.

Cancer is a shy bully. The gutters are filthy. I get a ladder and clean them.

Later I brush my hair in front of the fogged-up mirror, using the chewed-up hairbrush. In bed I listen to the dogs tapping against the kitchen tile. I yell through the bedroom door, "Lie down, for shit's sake."

"They must hear something outside," Miriam says.

"Of course they do," I say. "When do they not hear something? When do any of us not hear something somewhere—the sneaky rodent of life burrowing inside the clogged gutters of our subconscious! Shh. Listen. I can hear it right now."

"Oh, Lord in heaven. Is this because of your mommy dreams, Adelaide? Or because you can't think of anything smart to say in your book to win that old lesbian bitch's heart? Or because I'm dying? Why do you treat the world like a trash can?"

She gets out of the bed and laughs all the way to the kitchen. Suddenly Miriam is a satirist. There's nothing like the humor of a self-loving fat ass. I can hear her filling the water bowls. I'm sure she's rubbing the dog's heads, kissing them on the mouth. I hear the sliding glass door open as she lets them outside, where they can root around and investigate in their usual idiot manner. It's a while before she makes it back to bed. No doubt she fixed herself some food too. She should be losing weight, but she grows bigger. The wind outside is loud, and unusual. We're situated in a shallow valley. All around is the sound of a low, satisfied sigh.

PAGE TWENTY-THREE IN *Decker's Handbook of Gynecology for the General Practitioner*: "Menstrual abnormalities are frequent in the masculine female. Her pubic hair extends toward the umbilicus. She struggles to achieve sexual gratification, either alone or with her partner. In general, there is much hair, growing disobediently from her knuckles, her nape, and on and on as if trying to cover her, censor her in the face of civility. Her sexuality is a condition that must be corrected."

Decker wants to cure her, not merely for her own sake, obviously, but also for her restless husband's.

On a Saturday I cut words from antique medical records and arrange them into more potential chapter titles. Miriam leads the dogs on a walk up to the ridge. I have: "Hormone Girdle," "Manic Cervix," "Genital Apron." Miriam shows back up at the house almost four hours later, without her dogs. "I guess the dogs are out there trying to dig up an opossum. How's it going?"

"I think women have been trained to hate themselves. Also, they're moles," I say.

"Whatever," she says.

"Those bitches couldn't dig up a T-bone," I tell her.

"You might be onto something," she says.

"Your hormone girdle is too tight," I say.

When Miriam lies down for her nap I call Trisha to hear her raspy voice mail rumbling over the telephone. I unzip my jeans. I pull my underwear to the side. I can almost feel her staticky breath against my mouth. Her voice detonates me like a land mine. After I hang up I decide that when I finish the book I will dedicate it to Trisha. It will be for her, and, if done correctly, she will feel awe and affection toward it.

I nap too, and dream that Mother insists I seal the deal. "It's certainly a perfect trade," she says, "hell of an opportunity!" She is prodding forcefully with a wooden oar in a large metal trough full of corn. She moves the oar about as if she's rowing through it, like a little muddy pond. I move closer and realize that she's mixing a goat into the trough, covering it with corn. "We're backwoods," she says. "This is what we do. It took me a while to work out the details, but this should do it." She's making something in the trough. She insists I taste it. I do. I wake and I feel an enormous kind of relief that lasts for hours. I write until sundown.

There are small contradictions. They blemish the pages. I trace them angrily. It is certainly difficult to separate the body from its mannerisms, the shape and its performance, the origin of both. Does the hipbone make the lesbian? Or the lesbian make the hipbone? I resort to binaries: man/woman, penis/clitoris, angular/rounded, fertile/desolate, intelligent/overweight, ugly/overweight, old/young, dead/alive. Veracity is hinged to discomfort like a snake's jawbone to its skull. What good are we? Where are these confirmations of the parallels between the swells and reductions in one's passivity and dominance? I have convoluted the aim. I am trapped in a dumpster of possibilities.

AFTER SHE'D HEARD the voice in the barn that day, Mother knocked on Rupert's door. No one came. She knew they weren't home. There was no car in the driveway. She went back to the barn to finish shelling corn. She started feeding the corn into the crank again when she noticed that the bucket was swarming with wireworm larvae.

The larvae hadn't been there before she'd stepped outside. Someone started screaming. I explain to Miriam that the last time Mother told me this story over the phone, she stopped talking and I thought she'd hung up, until finally she yelled, "It was the man outside the barn, Adelaide, screaming for me! He wanted me! He wanted to kill me!"

"That makes sense," Miriam says. "Put that in your book."

"No," I say, "it doesn't."

MIRIAM SPENT THE day searching for the dogs. "Where could they have gone?" she asks.

"How would I know?" I say.

"Don't play dumb," she says, picking at a bit of food she's discovered on her blouse.

"Farewell," I say.

She weeps in her chair on the deck.

It was hours before Mother finally convinced her father to walk back over to Rupert's with her. He was a suspicious man, with an oily comb-over. They found a goat strung up in the electric fence, its mouth wide and stiff from screaming. "There's your ghost," her father said. For being such a bigot, Mother was very superstitious. It's obvious that the two are related.

In the recliner, looking out the picture window into the yard after dark, I imagine Mother running out of the woods, charging terrified through the leaves and tangled undergrowth. The trees are thick. When my mother was a girl, the house would have only been the single room I'm sitting in. Outside would have been the vaporous blue of a rural nightfall.

I have a handful of usable pages. I imagine each new word as a bacteria growing off the last. Writing about the body is suddenly an easy allegory about the ego. In last night's dream Mother was trying to pry open my fist. I was holding something. She said to me, "What if Miriam isn't dying?"

I woke abruptly to find Miriam standing over my bed. "Did you kill my dogs?" she asked.

"Shut up, Miriam," I said, still drugged with sleep, angry at her for the proxy sentimentality of these dreams.

We've been searching. We walked to the ridge and back four times. We made circles around the property. "Maybe they're just hiding," I say. Or maybe they have fled—from her flagrant mortality, with their dog instincts. Perhaps they are preparing for her death.

Miriam's face is half-lit under the yellow motion-sensor light above the porch. I expect the dogs to go running down the hill in front of the cabin, chasing a car, howling at the tires. But the country is quiet. Someone is headed toward town in an old pickup, kicking gravel dust up into a rolling cloud that drifts back over the yard like an enormous poltergeist in the moonlight. I ask her to come inside, please, but she says she can't. "Can you hear that? I hear barking," she says.

After I've been asleep for hours, she comes into my bedroom

again, saying, "If you go out by the shed you can smell them. I can smell the rotting flesh."

"Stop," I say.

"They've been gone so long they have to be dead and I can smell them. I hate this. I hate that they're gone. I have the right to bury them!"

"Your dogs are going to come back," I say. "They're out there eating shit right now." I open my arms and put her against me—a balloon on a pencil.

I look for the dogs again. I walk a mile in every direction, crisscrossing through the trees, calling out until I am hoarse. I can hear Miriam calling too.

I am walking east, up toward where the cliffs begin at the foot of the ridge, when I see them. At first I hope they're lying there asleep. I holler for them but sure as hell the fuckers are piled up like garbage, ugly and lumpy as old meat. Parts of them are scattered from where something has picked at them, the skin curled like paper around their rib cages. A knot rises. I sit there on the ground, staring. There is the stench, ripe and unfriendly. Mother refused to speak to me for a year after I told her I was gay. And after that she never mentioned it again. This is what I've inherited. A backwoods dream full of animals and dead homophobes. It is pungent and meager. It is homely, and hardly soothed by strange sex.

Miriam is sure I had something to do with it. We haul them back to the property in a wheelbarrow. I get the shovel from the garage and dig four holes while Miriam stands there petting the hard bodies. She steps back and I lift Trudy out of the wheelbarrow. Miriam says, "I want to lay them in there myself." So I let her. I don't want to touch them. The smell is stupid. She ties a shirt around her face and lowers each dog into her pit. I push the dirt back over the graves and then wait on the deck while she paints their names on scraps of plywood with some old paint she found in the shed. Of course the shovel is strange and heavy in my hands. She props the signs up in front of the mounds. She puts the boom box on the windowsill and plays her Eagles CD. I hide inside the house, holding X-rays up to the window, imagining what could have happened.

Probably Trisha will leave my life the same way she came in—an exotic snake crawling out of a toilet. Trisha is a dirt wasp trapped between a storm screen and a windowpane. Miriam is a magnolia in a bowl of water.

I dream Mother is walking with me to the garage. I give her shovel back to her.

"The dogs are dead," I say.

"No kidding?" she says.

"We buried them," I say.

"Sure," she says. "Good. I bet your lady is upset," she says.

"My lady?"

"Yeah, your woman. She's your woman now, ain't she? She's upset? But she's feeling better too, ain't she?"

I hand her the shovel and we go out into the yard. She wants to walk over to the dog graves, so I take her over and show them to her. She tells me to plant grass over the graves.

I say, "I might."

"Do it," she says, "or else you and your lady will have to look at this until the grass grows back on its own. And that'll be years from now."

IT IS THE self-devouring nature of theory—or maybe the road to resolve: A word appears, and then a sentence, and many ideas begin to take shape, then suddenly, more words, more theories. Some unwittingly cancel out preceding ones. Is the truest thing then left intact? When does the draft become a document? At some point every theorist will devastate herself. "One theory eats the other," I write across the title page of Chapter Three. And: "Learning is a ceremony in which we eat many possibilities only to crap them out again afterward." Just when you think you've proven something, you realize you've also opened yourself to the very opposite. One can locate me here, among the fallacies.

I HAVE ALREADY gone to bed when I hear Miriam humming to herself in the bathroom. I get up to check on her. I am in the kitchen and there, standing on the other side of the sliding glass door, is the lab, Trudy. I am sure. I have to cover my eyes. I hear the tap of a paw on the glass just as Miriam comes out of the bathroom. I look at her, then back at the door, but the dog is gone. "My head stopped hurting," Miriam says. "It's weird. I feel"—she hesitates—"better!" She begins to laugh uncontrollably, until tears are running down. When she catches her breath she asks, "What are you doing?" She must see the look on my face. "What's wrong?" she asks.

"I'm going outside," I say.

I stand on the deck, watching a low fog smothering the grass.

There is nothing, only the sound of an owl whooping somewhere beyond. I call out. I have a sensation of something electrical happening in my mouth. "Trudy!" I yell.

Miriam rushes out to stare at me. "What the fuck are you doing? God, you're a bitch. What is wrong?"

"I thought I saw something!" I yell back, my hands and head vibrating.

"SOME IDEAS MUST germinate for years," Trisha writes in the last chapter of *Morphologies and Eden.* "They take a lifetime to grow into something good and intricate. If you hold any idea underwater long enough it will start to break down, like a prisoner of war. Is this a good thing? Does the filthy husk fall away? The purest kernel left intact? A tortured prisoner will confess to anything. On the back of the oldest print of D568 I write, in very small print: "The body is the spirit's weakest echo."

In the Martian Summer

Her dear friend, Pauline, insisted there was something wrong. "Deeply wrong," was how she put it, in that administrative tone of hers. "Grave deep. Abyss deep!" Pauline carried herself with the passive authority of a politician's wife or a middle-income sex worker.

"Or maybe it's the moon," Mary Ann said, with a secret eye-roll. "The moon can have all sorts of odd effects on a person's psyche, Pauline! And that's science."

Pauline was no good at detecting sarcasm though. "I guess," she said, heading off alone in the dark toward her car.

Pauline was referring to the exotic vacation Mary Ann was about to embark upon. A handsome older gentleman wanted to take Mary Ann to the western coast of Mexico. He was going to teach her how to drive his yacht. Not a euphemism, Pauline! Ha. He actually owned a yacht. And honestly, the moon did hang low, perched like a colossal disk on the horizon, a bizarre amusement park attraction you could walk right up to if you wanted. Except Mary Ann didn't want to. She sat on the stoop in her knit shawl, watching silently as Pauline attempted for several minutes to unlock the wrong car.

How many times in her life had Mary Ann pretended to be interested in a ridiculous thing? And often for the attention of a ridiculous man. Of course it could all be traced back to her father, the original ridiculous man—more timeless wisdom from Pauline. Mary Ann's father had worked as a cartoonist, and naturally tended toward the goofier things in life. He'd asked Mary Ann to dress as a penguin while serving cocktails at his retirement party. She'd been the only person in a costume. But she did it for Daddy. He always had such affection for flightless birds, both in his work and personal life. Many family friends (old men) had patted Mary Ann on the ass during the party, fumbling awkwardly against the plush foam of the shortly cropped penguin suit. She was sixteen at the time, and felt obligated to endure most inappropriate attention.

Later, sans shawl, after Pauline had finally found the right car and drove away, the moon appeared blood-soaked—fatty and gristly as a tumor hovering over the twinkling city.

Recently there'd been a list of ridiculous excursions. A multiweek stint hanging around the Pony Palace Adult Theaters off I-70. Mary Ann was trying to be more open! An exhibitionist in charge of her own sexuality. To what improbable film plot did her days belong? A racy rom-com starring Goldie Hawn, that deranged platypus? Mary Ann had given hand jobs to several strangers. Eight. Who was counting? Partly she'd done it on account of her new cowboy friend, who she'd met in line-dancing class. And the whole adult theater idea had been the cowboy's. He was a total daydream to look at. Those hard arms. That worn-out hat. The shiny little snap buttons on his shirt. The Wranglers! He was a pure sweetheart. Until, of course, their last day together in the adult theater, during a showing of *Nympho Housewives III*. Mary Ann was performing a sort of two-handed lubricated maneuver on a particularly well-endowed construction worker when the cowboy bent down over her thrusting arm, opening his toothy mouth right as the construction worker began a seemingly endless release of ejaculate. Maybe that was also a sweetheart move. Except it broke her. She heard a popping sound somewhere inside her face. And it wasn't that the cowboy was interested in drinking semen. No. It was the other, stranger aversion he apparently had to touching a penis. Or telling her beforehand! My God. That this had been the goal all along. He'd encouraged her to perform hand sex on all these men just so he could locate the one with the most aggressive explosion. She had handled the young construction worker a week prior, and afterward, in the truck, the cowboy had gone on and on about it: "Man, what a load. He had it dripping off his chin. He almost got it in his mouth!" This announcement had been followed by an insane fit of laughter from the cowboy that sent chills up her arms.

In hindsight her foresight was terrible. That filthy, contortionist move, all so he could get a little sip. She felt a great sadness (sadness washed in annoyance) for people who longed to do an average thing but could not. Like have children, or get married, or wear a leash in public, or taste semen without ever laying hand or mouth to a penis. She couldn't bring herself to see him again after that. But she wanted to view it as a final lovely moment, so she decided to imagine him as a nervous baby bird waiting to be fed. She didn't want to cast herself as a victim either, though at her age it was so hard not to. She'd be forty soon. She was doing a multivitamin now, and it took double the number of squats and crunches to get the same results she'd achieved in her twenties. Growing old was hard, and naturally implied an inevitable state of victimhood.

After that, during an especially inebriated evening out with a real estate agent she'd met through 1-900-FUN-DATE, she badly wished she'd told the cowboy about her son. And her husband. A painful gloominess arrived in her chest as she and the real estate agent enjoyed their fruity cocktails, which had come served inside miniature watermelons. She'd meant to tell him—she'd wanted the cowboy to know he wasn't the only one with secrets, that she in fact had so many they were beginning to pile up. Sometimes at night she feared she might be buried beneath them. The problem was, with a secret you were alone, and it made her angry to think that he had used her to alleviate that loneliness. Because what was she left with? More secrets. After the cocktails she and the real estate agent went to a nightclub where, at some point during the night, she'd smoked crystal meth in the bathroom. Someone had fingered her too, in the handicapped stall, with the door wide open. And it wasn't the real estate agent, who, by the time it was all said and done, couldn't tell his fingers from his toes. She'd left him drooling on the street. Perhaps the whole evening was a wash? Her whole life, even? A wash. In acid.

Apparently Daddy wasn't the only one who gravitated toward the goofier things.

Why just one of these men couldn't be bright. Like a star or a headlight. Someone to guide her off the meandering rural route of her life.

But it was always something unsavory with single men these days. There were times—mainly on quiet afternoons, bored and sober in her quiet condo—when she worried the problem might be her. Perhaps some crucial function in her brain had shorted out as a result of . . . a result of what? Being alive?

She desperately needed something simpler, something lighter and brighter than the greedy, black reptile sidewinding through her body most days, that twisted polluted river deep inside her, threatening to drown her nearly every moment of her fucking life.

She lived in Colorado, for God sakes! How did that even happen? Among the flashy mountains and constant pothead tourists. When would she ever need to know how to drive a damn yacht?

Yet, it appealed to her.

She imagined which outfit she would wear while manning the elegant helm. She was leaning toward a pale blue sweater-and-shorts set from Land's End. Also she was mulling over her little bartender's handbook, trying to determine which obscure cocktail she might enjoy while sailing those vast glittering waters broken only by the wake of the pristine ship charging to Chile, maybe, or Antarctica.

The man with the yacht was Cuban. He wore large horn-rimmed glasses that framed his milk-gray eyes like two small, sad photos. He also sported a gold watch, and rarely wore socks. He did something with oil and gas, living out of hotels for several months of the year—another thing that appealed to her.

It used to be that, years ago, she'd had a specific type, which was really just any man who reminded her of her dead husband. Apparently Bill had set a kind of precedent, activating in her a predilection for dense body hair, a meaty thickness, a Neanderthal forehead, a stiff gait that didn't allow the arms to make contact with the body when he walked. Bill had been a foreman in the coal mines at La Plata County. He'd had such an easy laugh, and a clownish tendency of being overly polite. It wasn't as if she encountered men like this all the time, but any one of those things reminded her of another. The traits seemed related. As if huge foreheads were closely linked to a peculiar ability to laugh, sincerely, even when nothing funny had been said. Biology was weird.

Come back, Bill, she often thought to herself, alone in the bathrooms of the places she attended with these new men, come back now or else I might die too. With my head pressed against the cold, dirty stall of some random public toilet.

But then again, absolutely not. Stay dead, Bill. Please stay dead. It wasn't uncommon for her to be walking down the street and think, for a burning second, that she saw Bill rushing toward her with some alarming purpose, until the man turned, with that witless smile, to enter some store or side street, slipping out of view again. "Just take a moment to imagine the nightmarish heartache this conjures in me!" she'd exclaimed to Pauline. Each time it happened she felt unhinged for hours. She always likened it, after the fact, to the sensation of some space-age material capable of turning from solid to liquid in an instant. When it occurred she did her best to rush home, pop a Xanax, and lie down face-first on the kitchen tiles.

"Keep an open mind, Mary Ann!" Pauline would say. "Imagine a world where the dead really do live among us. These sightings could be a miraculous thing! Think of it like this: Bill will always be nearby."

Unfortunately, mental breakdowns ran in both her and Pauline's families, so neither's perception could be trusted.

SEVERAL MILES OFF the coast of Nayarit, on the bow of the great white ship, she stood next to the Cuban, each of them holding in their hands a shockingly emerald-colored drink. It tasted foul, like licorice mixed with perfume. But, oh, how it looked when held out against the near-blue churning and the smoother sea beyond. Like something from a movie. The Cuban had paid for the whole excursion, thank God. Because even though she'd been prepared to pay her own way, she did not want to—news of the lavish vacation had caused more than one nasty interaction with Pauline, who'd basically begged Mary Ann for money the month before. Mary Ann had respectfully declined, if only because she felt Pauline lived beyond her means, a habit that caused all affection for Pauline to leak like fuel from the iron tank of Mary Ann's heart. Helping others was so hard sometimes. Even devoted Pauline. Being friends with a person for over twenty years didn't just entitle them to a portion of your hard-won assets!

While considering this, even perhaps beginning to feel a little guilty, the crystal drink carafe slid off the edge of its little marble table and, before she could manage to catch it, fell and shattered against the smooth wooden deck. She jumped back just in time to avoid getting her new sandals wet. The whole yacht began to pitch itself rapidly, and the small man whom they'd hired to oversee the yachting lesson put his hands up to his leathery face and started screaming. Mary Ann jerked her head in every direction, in front of the ship, and behind, before finally realizing that from the east rose a blistering white wall of water. It was hard to understand what was happening, at first. Was it abnormal activity? Mary Ann removed her expensive sunglasses to get a better look, and all at once it came into focus: A giant shimmering hellscape was charging patiently toward them. "I knew the water was rising!" the tiny bronze captain called out, more to himself than to anyone aboard. "I fucking knew it."

The initial moments after this passed in horrible silence—except for a strange onslaught of pale birds anxiously squawking overhead, scattering across the sky like thin material fluttering toward the coast. These seabirds released a detached panic in Mary Ann. The Cuban reached out and took her hand, immediately gathering her in his hulky arms, tightly pressing her back against the barrel of his chest. He began kissing the back of her head too. His lips were in her hair. This disgusted Mary Ann. She thought he might be crying though, so she allowed it until he whispered, "I will keep you safe, Mary." He pronounced it "Marie." As his breath hit her neck she couldn't help but envision his gruesome death: the boat snapping in half under the force of the coming wave, the deck opening up like a jaw, gnawing him into two purple halves.

Finally the captain called down, instructing them to retrieve their life jackets and buckle themselves onto the bench. "What is it? What's happening?" Mary Ann demanded, her voice cracking as the Cuban tossed the bench's wicker throw pillows overboard.

"We're going to try to outrun the worst of it," the Cuban said. "He'll survey the surge," he assured her, "and should be able to determine with some accuracy the speed at which the water is traveling."

"If we move fast enough," the captain yelled, "we will not meet the wave until after it breaks! There will be turbulence," he said, "but little damage."

"Damage!" Mary Ann shrieked. Her anxiety mutated into raddled fury.

He'd already turned the boat around and they were heading toward a crooked bundle of islands to the west. Against her better judgment, she turned again to face the rising swell. For a moment the wave blended with the empty sky, making the two barely distinguishable—an ill-focused blue sheet—until it rolled back in on itself, exposing another roaring progression of whitecaps. She looked down at her hands. She'd worn too many rings, she realized, and was still clutching the gaudy drink. The broken glass of the carafe was splayed around her feet, the shards jittering on the polished wood. Many gross fantasies occurred to her as they sped past the rocky islands, every new vision smeared with the image of her companions' slippery blood.

The Cuban was calling up to the captain, attempting to discuss something that Mary Ann could not bring herself to digest—rules for how best to swim in violent waters. Her mind blinked off way before any of that. If it came down to it, she decided quickly, she would only be able to surrender. She felt her body go slack at the thought. She focused instead on the growing sight of the rolling wall as it stretched out the entire length of the visible sea. It was almost close enough now, she thought, for her to locate objects within it. Each time something came into view, though, she decided it was just the movement of darker water inside the wave. It was still less than a mile away, but shapes continued to appear and recede: a cluster of fins, smaller boats, cumbersome plant life, and then, with a hot glitch of nausea, human bodies. She made a sound, or must have, because the Cuban turned to look at her, putting his heavy arm around her shoulders. "What is it, Marie?" he said. She was certain she'd misunderstood the contents of the wall. When she met his eyes, she noticed the glass inside his flamboyant frames was speckled neatly with condensation. The lenses were as fake as his beautiful teeth. Where the hell was she? She was certain she could detect a helpless dread in his eyes, even as he worked to conceal it.

"Marie, just look at me. You can only look at me. If we have to leave this boat for any reason I will stay by you."

"Yes," she said, knowing that if they did go overboard, each of them would immediately be separated by the grinding undercurrent.

Minutes passed with her only looking at the Cuban's arms

and the wiry black hair that escaped his collar. She touched her fingernail to the little dog embroidered on the breast of his bright shirt. She was unable to turn back to the water at all now, though part of her still longed to observe its lagging approach. She understood it might be her only chance, in all her life, to see something so dangerous and extraordinary. It felt foolish not to pay attention, but her body would no longer allow it. The same weakness that had pushed her to abandon the initial prospect of swimming through all that boiling water was the same weakness that kept her from turning to monitor the towering blast. She was vibrating at her very core, and so was the boat. If they had to jump ship, what idiot would attempt to beat out the power of the ocean? Wouldn't it be smarter to just give in? To hold one's breath and pray your body bobbed to the surface? Like a corpse.

She was cursing aloud now, though the Cuban tried to keep her calm. It was obvious to her in an instant: Any day of the week the earth could tear you in half like a wet sheet of paper. And yet somehow people continued to assert their authority over it. And often succeeded.

"I never told my family I was going on this trip," the Cuban whispered.

"What? Where are they? Your mom and dad?" she asked, putting her hand up to his face.

"Florida. But I meant my wife and children."

"You're married?" she asked.

"I thought you knew," he said.

Maybe she did know. She took her hand away. If she didn't look at the water, it was possible to assume they were merely traveling at a high speed for the sport of it. She didn't care if he was married, though knowing he was thinking of his wife and children made her feel unsafe. An inherent moral ambivalence had kept her resilient these past few years, if not a little disjointed, at times, from the world around her. If he had informed her of his wife, she'd simply forgotten it, like a middle name or a birthday.

She was somewhere else anyway, dying a little, thinking, somehow, of a massive arch-shaped dam that Bill had taken her to see many years ago.

It must have been late into the pregnancy with Danny. She'd felt beastly and weighed down and groggy the entire trip and after touring the dam's powerhouse, where the rumbling generators were kept, she'd immediately wanted to return to the hotel. What dickery of mind it'd taken to imagine this monolithic stone cup, halved and slipped right into the mountain's basin, holding back all that placid water on the other side. Tons! Of water, and dickery. Men were so cocky. Yet it was a perfectly tuned monstrosity, providing electricity to half the state. Why *was* it so terrifying? When Bill had died in the mines, like so many other stupid men on the western slope, she'd obsessed for months, when she wasn't catatonic, over how egotistical the entire industry was for even attempting such an extraction in the first place. Years spent gutting the abyss of the ground like a giant gourd. Of course it was going to crush them: much of the work they did was to keep it all from caving back in around them every step of the way. The rage she felt for seemingly commonplace things had only multiplied over the years. It'd always sort of been there.

The moment she'd gotten the phone call from Pauline, saying there'd been another accident in the mine, and there were deaths—she knew, somehow. Or maybe she'd thought it before and this time it happened to be true? Either way, it was a hammer striking against her skull, rattling loose some previously unreachable materials. Lost memories lobbed briefly to the surface. Seemingly ancient griefs dislodged themselves. Her unknown self was cracked into countless pieces—she could try to name them now, those separate aspects she'd glimpsed during the initial shock, but the list was so damn long it was hard to keep track. And besides, hadn't every facet of her self first risen out of an unnamable, primitive darkness?

Even water could be infinitely divided, she thought now, with a blinding pinprick.

It was as if there were no true senses. Every knowable thing was contingent on the next catastrophe, causing all of her ideas to morph into a flat, numb rage toward any system she could not easily comprehend. And there were so many.

She didn't get to see his body. Recovery efforts were pointless. He was still down there. In what state of decay, or transformation, she often wondered.

And even here speeding on the water her head was swamped with morbid visions, one a repeating scene in which she opened her mouth wide enough to lunge savagely at the Cuban's face, biting off his nose. She clenched her teeth and tried not to imagine the hot, tart blood filling her mouth. The salt water on her lips didn't help. She thought of the flesh breaking as she bit. It was true she'd grown impulsive, and that the impulsivity had assumed control over her. Every moment had the potential of becoming a gruesome hallucination, and the impending wave confirmed it. She looked out ahead of the yacht to see that they were passing another island. She could see a half-submerged building, shingled roofs, and the upper floor of a meager apartment where the shapes of people shifted in the windows. She called out to the captain to ask where the wave was, but he did not respond. He extended his thin hand instead, insisting she wait.

So much time passed. It was unreal, she thought, how much could be contained in a moment. Just as it occurred to her though, off in the developing distance she could discern a rugged gray sliver of coastline on the horizon.

It was on a recent trip alone to Dallas, in a packed midtown bar, where Mary Ann had joined a group of Egyptian investors in their VIP booth and fallen into a swoon of flashing lights before allowing each of them to dance with her. Their accents had been so charming, and indecipherable. They'd bought her drinks. She followed them to an after-party a few blocks away. In a cramped bedroom Mary Ann took a hit of pot. Her words slurred into drivel. Perhaps one of them had actually carried her to the house? And she had not walked? Another couple, with terrible smiles, came into the bedroom too. It was their house, she understood later. The woman took Mary Ann's purse and rifled through it. "Candy or gum, sweetie pie?" the woman had asked. Mary Ann found it hard to sit up. The loud hostess bared her rotten set of teeth as she dumped out the contents of Mary Ann's purse.

When she woke the next morning, in the grassless backyard of the ugly house, there was a fiery discomfort between her legs and the flickering memory of a harsh, duplicitous entering. Also, the unbelievable memory of the hostess sitting heavy and bare-assed on Mary Ann's face.

Now the woman was standing at the back door, glaring. "What the fuck are you doing in my yard, lady? Do I need to call the cops?"

Mary Ann attempted to stand, but her legs weren't working. "Why did you let them do that?" she'd asked.

"Excuse me?" the woman said, with a hand cupped to her ear.

Mary Ann hadn't used her full voice, so she asked again, "Why did you let them do that to me?" Maybe it was the dead look on the woman's face, or maybe Mary Ann was in shock, but she began to weep hysterically, screaming as loud as she could, "I'm a mother!" She was saying it to the woman, but also to anyone within earshot. Who knows why she did it. Later she would only feel embarrassed, still hearing the sound of her own idiot voice ringing out in the dusty backyard—a desperate moron's call for compassion: *I'm a mother, I'm a mother, I'm a mother!*

It had given the woman pause, but only for as long as it lasted. The woman looked around to see if anyone had noticed, then recomposed her empty gaze. "Get out of my yard, you ugly bitch. You're trespassing," she said. She'd slammed the door, causing a little, rusted cowbell to fall dully down each step, landing in the dirt.

Mary Ann hung closer to other women for a couple of weeks

after that, even invited two baristas from the coffee shop over to her house for a movie night. They'd both cheeringly accepted, then never showed. Something had been lifted from her, and she wanted it back. She even went as far, on a night out with Pauline, as leaning in close on the sidewalk, cheek to cheek, clutching Pauline's soft hand before impulsively attempting to engage her in an intimate kiss. Pauline had pulled back almost immediately. "Mary Ann! Are you lesbian now?" she'd yelled.

Mary Ann had responded with explosive laughter, which seemed to shock Pauline even further. "I've never done it. Have you? It just seems like everyone else is doing it!" Mary Ann cried.

"I have not. I mean, I kissed Claudia Comber once in the bathroom at the Skate Palace in junior high. But not as an adult!"

This statement had caused Mary Ann to fall into a severe crying jag. Pauline had to take her home and put her to bed. Claudia Comber, my God, Mary Ann had thought, what a homely troll.

OCCASIONALLY SHE COULD hold an entire day like warm liquid in the perfect pool of her palms. Other days crackled under her skin with a fiery static, a nearly intolerable restlessness—those were the moments that seemed to arrest her, to hold her captive like a prisoner in a confusing war.

But this was different. This day wanted to devour her completely.

Maybe thirty minutes after they'd spotted the wave, the yacht was washed ashore—the sleek vessel shoved out of the sea like it was nothing at all, airy driftwood. Mary Ann crouched down in her seat and covered her head. Water came at her from all directions, filling her nose, soaking her clothes. The Cuban held her the entire time, tight as a fist, bruising up her arms. And even though she could not see, she could feel the yacht's engine cut out and the stomach-dropping shift in momentum that sent them hurtling toward what used to be a beach. There was the racket of debris all around them, street stands and furniture and mopeds and toppled trees. The collision was the truest thing, she thought, when she finally stood up and looked around—it was always the afterward for her, and not the during, where things made sense.

Her feet stung and she could see that her heels had been cut by the broken carafe. The wave had met them and sent them rushing over the foam. The wide parking lots and swimming pools and cabanas were all submerged. Much of the coast they had walked along together when they first arrived was now underwater. The yacht was wedged between a small restaurant and a Marriott Hotel. People were screaming down at them from the floors overhead, in another language, but one that she understood, saying, "Are you hurt? How many of you are there?" Terrible things gushed by: the gutted remains of other boats, trash and animals—a person floating, the clothes ballooning out around the open arms, the hair swirling like a burst of ink around a lilac-colored head. She felt a sick sense of relief, and then shame. They had escaped, in a clumsy instant. Other people had not. The way the yacht had been propelled, the way it slid into place among the buildings, the way the Cuban and the captain were searching for objects to stand on so that they might reach a nearby window in the wall of the hotel because water was filling the boat—if you looked at it a certain way, the ocean had merely moved forward a bit, less than a mile. If you looked at it another way, something apocalyptic had occurred, and she had survived. There were several snapped-off planks of wood protruding from the muddy water beside the yacht, like a single row of giant ribs, and in her mind Mary Ann was impaling herself on them over and over.

"We have to climb out right now," the captain said.

They stacked three metal coolers on top of one another, in order to reach the window where a greasy man waited, his arms outstretched and ready to haul them through. The leaves of the still-standing trees twitched and Mary Ann could see through the lush foliage. Legions of frantic birds crowded the limbs. Their calls were belligerent. The Cuban insisted she enter first. They were all sweating, humidity pressing on them like a hot, pissy blanket as they lifted Mary Ann into the stranger's arms. Her expensive sandals dropped from her feet as he wrapped himself around her, dragging her into the room, scraping her thighs up on the sill.

The others climbed in while Mary Ann sat panting on the still-made bed, listening to the man explain that there had been an earthquake. Two of them. The first one happened inland, the second one at sea. "The first earthquake broke all the bridges," he said, once everyone was inside. "And the second one caused the tidal wave."

"Tsunami," the Cuban corrected him, loudly, as he searched the bathroom for towels. "Technically speaking!"

They all looked up, and then at the floor. He stuck his head out of the bathroom, wiping the dirt and sweat from his face with some tissue paper. "Since it wasn't caused by the tide?"

"Yes," the other man said. "Okay. I have Coke from the vending machine. Would you want one? There aren't many. We are only waiting now, hoping there won't be more activity."

"Yes," they all said.

Mary Ann was extremely thirsty.

The whole event was a forced reconstitution of time, she decided, sitting on the edge of the tub, trying to comprehend. It had been minutes at most, from their first sighting of the wave until it ran them aground. But it stretched out in her mind: a bounty of realities located in a single sideways span. There had been many occasions in the last couple of years when death had seemed so simple and correct. She licked a thumb, trying to wipe dirt from the cuts on her feet and legs. Often, in the stillest hours of evenings before this, staring at the walls in her condo, she felt she could hear the universe buzzing, signaling a glowing hunger to extinguish her. She was only waiting for it. The very particles of her body had sped up in an attempt to process the doom of the wave. She could assess it now, inside the raucous hotel, as the people on the upper floors carried on loudly, waiting for emergency relief to arrive or the water to recede or for other tremors to follow. A man went door to door, saying that the authorities would probably send helicopters or boats to rescue those who'd been trapped. Within hours insects were swarming in droves, covering the windows, their tiny brown bodies flicking ecstatically against the glass. They put a sheet over the door to keep them from crawling in through the cracks. There was no power, but still a constant distressful noise outside. When darkness began to fall, every sound set her on edge. Mary Ann requested a second soda, which she drank slowly, while the men filled plastic cups with water from the back of the toilet tank. The waiting was excruciating, though the captain kept insisting that if there were going to be another earthquake, it would have already occurred.

Mary Ann did not agree. All night the smell of the men in the room woke her. She'd fallen into a less panicked state during sleep, the panic replaced by a circuitous burning that whirred in the pit of her stomach, drowning out every other emotion—her whole existence narrowed to an X-rated pinhole. In her dreams the sweat-drenched men came to her, and she welcomed them, as if fulfilling her anatomical destiny, receiving all three of them at once. They rotated around her like a powerful, slick machine, filling every hole. She woke with her hand in her shorts, the dream still lingering on her as she reached over in the dark, feeling for whoever was next to her. It was the Cuban, she was sure, running her hand through his chest hair. Before the sun came up she'd coaxed him into the bathroom, leaving the door open, hoping the others would come in as well. They did not. But by the time it was over she was grateful they hadn't. It wasn't an entirely erotic situation. The room turned sour. Her feet ached from the cuts and a thin horn whined from one of the floors beneath. The Cuban had wept. He'd mentioned his wife again, even though Mary Ann made the considerate gesture of bending herself over the sink so he could get at her from behind. When that didn't work, she'd finished herself off by grinding against his stubby, shaky fingers. Was she in charge of anything at all? What power did *she* have over the world? She had wanted to comfort him, in a way, but also it was hard to feel anything but revulsion toward the sobbing.

Lying at the end of the bed, staring at the green-lit window, she felt drugged. She was an animal in distress. Didn't it always seem like the most natural course of action, though? Until it was over. In hindsight, the majority of her sex longings called to mind the image of a person climbing out of quicksand, or crawling out of her own loose skin in an attempt to escape the hot slop of her messy insides. She could still smell the Cuban on her, and it made her stomach turn. The smell of him reminded her of a food item she'd once eaten and not enjoyed.

After the sun began to streak across the murky room, with its odor and edginess, she started to worry that Pauline would hear the news about the earthquakes and become hysterical. When she was home, Mary Ann decided, she would attempt a more patient friendship with Pauline.

The men went out again to help clear debris from the stairwells and Mary Ann hid in the bathroom with the door locked, dipping a washcloth into the back of the toilet. They'd be upset with her for using the only drinking water, but it felt so good, and eased her, knowing her face and vagina were clean. She used a drop of scented shampoo on the cloth too.

She was certain that Pauline would see the whole ordeal as a kind of punishment. "Don't you see the relationship?" she'd plead—as if a person's deeds were balloons pushed underwater, inevitably popping up at crucial points along the surface of a life. Good grief, Pauline, always such a know-it-all, even at the worst of times, when all a person needed was compassion!

Mary Ann would make sure to stress, again, that she had not paid for the trip.

It was true that Pauline had been extremely willing during those stupefying months after Bill's death. She'd been the only one helping Mary Ann care for Danny. He was four years old and cried almost constantly. Somehow Bill and Pauline had never minded spoon-feeding the boy, but Mary Ann refused. What sort of precedent did it set, she'd ask, as Danny flung himself on the floor, smearing his body in oatmeal.

After Bill's funeral the fantasies arrived. Like a sack of soothing demons on the doorstep, transmitting images into her brain for hours on end. The worst of them: snatching Danny from his playpen and throwing him against the living room wall. Also, on the days when Pauline was gone, filling the child's drink cup with sedatives. What had stopped her? The thought of being ostracized, or imprisoned?

She'd made a habit of observing the starlings on the power lines outside the bathroom window, after several whiskey and waters. All day, whiskey and water. This had helped. With all of the kid's problems, being alone with him, without Bill, her body switched off, like a fuse in a house with too many appliances running at once. A baby, a child at all, was never something she'd wanted. She knew this like she knew all of her aversions—that she hated bluegrass music, and eggplant, and badly behaved dogs. He'd been for Bill. And with Bill gone, what was the point? Suddenly the idea of an animal eating its offspring seemed perfectly natural. She was surprised it didn't occur more often. But how to say this, in a world full of women dying to be somebody's mother?

Where was there room for her to grieve? There was a savage in her midst. He'd swallow small toys whole, hardly blinking. The looks of the emergency room staff became intolerable. For someone else, maybe, this kind of calamity could have been a distraction, but for her the two nightmares played out in unison, folding over each other, enclosing her. She hid in the garage, pretending to search for some lost thing while Danny howled on the kitchen floor, lost in the frenzy of a tantrum. If she did try to approach him, he'd kick her, spit in her face. If she went to another room to escape, he'd follow her, beating his head and fists on the door until she let him in, so that he could continue the fit at her feet. He demanded a witness. Once she found him on the neighbor's outdoor patio, smacking himself in the mouth, blood dripping down his chin. During a family barbecue! He rarely spoke to her. Only a universe that prided itself on manifold sicknesses, on its own ironic design, would offer something so unlovable to someone so unmaternal.

Rather than bashing in his head, though, she retired to the bathroom, where she crushed up her anxiety medication into smooth, perfect lines that she snorted off the bathroom sink with a straw.

"Come out of that bad place, Mother!" she would say to herself in the mirror. "Transform! Wake up!"

But she couldn't.

When she had truly given up and arranged for Danny to move into a facility, the world, begrudgingly perhaps, seemed to right itself. There was shame, sort of, but also peace. The peace was louder. The house droned in commiseration. It was as if a hole had opened, causing a great pressure to escape her. A giant cork had been removed. And there was a place for everything now, for everyone, to come in and fill her up again. She did visit him, on some weekends, at first, until the director of the facility advised her to stop.

People who you loved were simply with you and alive, and then they were not. How does one move forward? It depended on who you were, she guessed, as to which method one might use. At first, her only desire was to lie down on a clean sofa somewhere, one that didn't reek of human urine. But then other things presented themselves, generously.

On the afternoon following the day of the earthquakes, as Mary Ann and the others sweated it out in their room, announcements of an official rescue began to circulate. Mary Ann and the men shared a small bag of pork rinds, even played tic-tac-toe, passing the sheet of paper and the snack around in a circle. They could hear what sounded like instructions over a megaphone, being given to the occupants of an apartment building farther up the beach. The captain kept going to the window, hanging his head out, trying to hear. The smells unleashed each time he lifted the glass were ripe with salt and rot.

Maybe, in the end, she was grateful for Danny's condition. It had given her a reason to flee. Ages later, it felt, she'd risen from that disgusting season, that double nightmare, into a new body, replete with a stylish condo from all the insurance money.

Right before she'd left on the trip, hours before she was scheduled to be at the airport, she and Pauline had met for lunch, to say goodbye and for Mary Ann to leave a key to the condo. Pauline was going to turn on some lights at night and water the only houseplant—a bromeliad that tolerated neglect so well Mary Ann hardly watered it herself. It was unnecessary, but Pauline wanted to be useful. Good old Pauline.

The argument, if you'd even call it that, came out of nowhere, right after the food was served. Pauline laid both of her hands on the table and said, "He tells me things."

"What?" Mary Ann had said, still chewing. She truly despised Pauline the most for things like this. "Who? Who tells you things, Pauline?"

"Danny, when I go to the facility to see him, or when we talk on the phone, which isn't often really, on the phone, because he gets excited. Oh, his speech has improved, Mary Ann, enormously."

"What in the hell are you talking about?" Mary Ann had hissed, driving her knife deep into the meat on her plate, causing the pink juice to puddle around her steamed vegetables.

"Mary Ann, you wanted to know and so I'm telling you."

"I did? When did I ever say such a thing?"

"The loan would have been for him," Pauline said, looking down at her tuna cakes. This was how Pauline approached every difficult situation, lowering herself, pretending to be humble in all her endless judgement. "It's getting so expensive to drive out there, Mary Ann, and you know they don't provide for everything he needs. They send me home with a list every time. But it's not like I mind. I do not mind. I just haven't been working as much."

"I hope you understand," Mary Ann had said, clutching her cutlery, "that I see this as a total betrayal. Who told you to visit him? It goes against policy."

"Oh, stop." Now Pauline was waving a hand, acting like it was nothing. "A child just needs familiars. That's all. You know? I couldn't stand the thought of him not seeing a friend. He's taking classes now. Math, science. The other day he called just to tell me about Mars! Isn't that funny? Like I'd never heard of Mars. He gets excited. He actually said, 'Do you know about Mars?' I laughed and laughed. Fascinating stuff. You never get too old to learn!"

Mary Ann could only hone in on the blood floating across her plate, how it made islands out of her side dishes. The steak was too rare. Sweat was pouring down her spine, dampening the back of her blouse. The knife upon the soiled napkin suddenly seemed to her like the most poignant thing she'd ever witnessed.

"It was the seasons on Mars that really got him. Did you know other planets have seasons? It's common knowledge, I guess. And I mean, it makes sense, but maybe it wouldn't occur to everyone. 'I'll spend summers on Mars!' he said. He knows that isn't possible. He just liked saying it. He does that, repeating things. I had to get off the phone because he wouldn't stop yelling."

Apropos of the whole ordeal, a light snow had begun to fall outside the restaurant. Mary Ann's seat was facing the window. The weather enraged her. It wasn't even winter yet. Much of the snow melted before it hit the pavement.

"I can't wait for the damn sunshine," Mary Ann said, nodding toward the street. "I've always felt I was more suited to a tropical climate."

"A Martian summer is still just dead-cold. Cold upon cold," Pauline continued.

Mary Ann could not bring herself to entertain another word. She thought of Mexico instead, of the Cuban and his expensive yacht.

"Not as cold as it is the rest of the time, though. It's the strange mixture of gases, I think, that do it. You think you've got it bad, Mary Ann? Those are seriously harsh conditions!"

Mary Ann was certain she already knew this information. From school? From Bill? Something about how there were no bodies of water to retain the heat? No oceans, no beaches. Regions of Mars, even in summer, were still cold enough to crack your bones. Pauline could be such a condescending bitch. "Pauline, you condescending bitch," Mary Ann finally said, the knife somehow back in her hand, thrusting forward. "Everyone knows all of this." She had to put Pauline in her place. She had to stop the onslaught of hostility!

"Please put down the knife," Pauline had said.

But before Mary Ann had walked outside to wait for her cab

in the snow, leaving Pauline alone at the table with her fish, she'd added, harshly, "You're not a mother, Pauline. But just imagine you were, and imagine you could choose to do something else instead. And suddenly the world opened its arms to you! And strangers wanted to take you to explore remote and exotic locations. It'd be a sweet, wonderful day and I'd be happy for you. I'd celebrate!"

Of course now, in the rank hotel, she wished she hadn't said any of that, and not just because the days that had followed seemed like a kind of punishment after all, like a snarky reckoning. But because it wasn't the point. In the sickening hotel room, waiting and waiting, she played the conversation over in her head, wishing she'd said something else entirely, something like, "Listen, old friend, there is no way in hell a Martian summer is harsher than all of this!"

Gordon Now

Every day now Gordon is somewhere: standing in the hallway with his hands in his pockets when I flick on the overhead light, ducking quickly into the water-heater cabinet, pulling the little door shut behind him. Sometimes I whisper from the other side, "What are you doing?" But he doesn't say anything and when I open the door he's gone. Other days I'll go out to start the car in the morning and he's lying faceup in a snowdrift by the driveway, just staring up at the dark sky. When I go out again later, the sun is coming up and he's gone again. He'd find it funny, I'm sure, how uncomfortable I get. He'd probably say, "Stop acting like a girl." He was always trying to scare me and shit. Now he's dead. And I'm left with this.

When he first disappeared it felt like I was lodged in a narrow pipe, stuck like a clog, waiting to be flushed—and then, months later, like I was dead too, a shriveled-up corpse inside another bigger corpse, trying to find my way out. Grief builds up around me like plaque.

The whole time, people kept saying he'd run off to Chicago

or Bowling Green with some girl, or his dealer. Gordon wasn't someone you could count on. But I knew. Somehow.

Now the fucking *van kids* come and drag me out into the cold to party all night. "It's a proper funeral!" they say. "A fun one! We have to do it, for Gordon! You need this." Like they're trying to help. It's an excuse to use drugs. Everything is.

We head out into the country, where someone's parents own a cabin and a giant barn. From the stables to the barn doors there is dancing. Everywhere is the smell of animals and animal waste. The barn looks like it's been cleaned, but the smell lingers. Someone has tied a bubble machine to a rafter and it fills the air around us with trembling orbs. We haven't been here ten minutes and for some reason I'm grinding, half-assed, against this Persian chick I hardly know from Steelville.

Eventually, I do some back flips—straight up and then down. I almost land in the spot where I jumped. Everyone has cleared a spot for me. The Persian chick gets swallowed by the crowd like a weak drink. The subwoofers are covered in forty ounces. I wonder if I could down them all. When the spotlights rise, I watch the liquid shudder inside the bottles. The synthesizers are squealing and the sound lights up the stables—all red and smoldering. "Holy shit," someone says, and then I'm pressed between all these fucking people, standing on my toes to see what's going on. I take someone's Olde English from the speaker. A tablet has settled in it—*almost dissolved*. I can see the last orange bit. The "holy shit" was about me, I realize— someone going on about the flip. I just tip the bottle and gulp, taking even the hot froth. The strobe lights go quick and a giant bubble descends like a glass planet—impaled tenderly on a glow stick.

I wonder how I'll get home.

I watch through a circular window as the snow blasts across the harvested fields. Reflecting in the glass, over the cut rows, a mirror ball revolves. Finally, I break a fucking sweat.

They found Gordon three days ago, after years of searching, and then not searching anymore. His bones and teeth, at least— every piece covered in bright algae. They showed his mother a photo of the spot. They offered her the remains. She called me and told me to go get them. "They're yours," she said. "That doesn't make any sense," I said, but she was like, "You damn well know it does." She hung up on me. The body was not a body anymore. What was it? A joke told incorrectly? A handful of glowing stones?

Or something. *Go figure*—he was always saying this, meaning he expected bad things to happen. And pretty much they did.

Girls bounce by—tits, big asses—their slick ponytails pivoting behind them like the tails of actual ponies. What else? The Marishi sisters pop and lock on a speaker box wrapped in blue Christmas lights. Their expressions match—bitchy—and their limbs glitch in unison. Some punk in an arm cast fakes a sweep drop near the kegs. The other people here are totally gone. Only their sweaty bodies are left, shiny and empty as athletes.

I hide beside the fog machine, freestyling, trying to lose myself. I used to be able to do that. I attempt a couple of air flares. When I open my eyes the girlie boys have huddled around me like pets. Like they want something.

Gordon was a terrible dancer. He didn't know what to do with his arms. His body flailed. He could fight though, and somehow was graceful as an animal at it.

"You don't come to the Shoe Factory anymore," the boys say, bumping hips, one after the other in a long row, before sending it back again in the opposite direction. "The kid on the Wavetable tonight is serious. Too bad it's a Yamaha. That's fucked-up about Gordon," they say.

Man, they're rags, downers.

That they would even say his name, it splatters like poison.

"My buddy says it's probably not Gordon," the one in red glasses confides. "He says it's some hippie who drove his car into the strip pit five years ago."

Fuck you. What do you know? Everyone wants to siphon the grief out. They can't suck hard enough. It never rises to the surface.

I just stare at their made-up faces, balancing the empty beer bottle on my fingers before I fling it, *stunningly, really*, into a garbage can a few yards away. I squint at the boys. The coils of the portable heaters glow like little burning fences, corralling everyone.

Someone says, "My brother has a Yamaha, dude. Shit sounds like Phil Collins giving anal-birth to Celine Dion!" Their laughter is thin and sharp as a pocketknife.

"What's wrong with Collins?" I ask. I've interrupted the joke. They're trying to refigure their taste now.

I should leave. I should catch a ride back into town, head into the snow and wait for this pill to kick in. Tonight the world is an icy eyehole. I want to crawl inside it, I want to burrow in it, to be so cold it burns. But, I see Gordon here too. Damn, and he's climbing onto the speaker box with the Marishi sisters. He wedges himself between them. Or creases? Or has grown there, all of a sudden, in that *infinitesimal* fucking *space* between their bodies. It's like Gordon owns them. He's grinning a big ol' clown grin, because he thinks girls love to get owned. He gives them both a leg so they can ride him—two kids mounting a seesaw. The Marishis are trying to climb Gordon like a little ladder.

All three of them flicker like an evil robot before the strobe— a single human engine on the verge of *total fucking transformation*—turning more and more monstrous between the stabbing segments of light.

Something is happening with the pill.

Over the throb of the bass beat, one of the girlie boys, the one with rhinestones glued to his face, yells, "Who's your ride? You drive out here?"

Shut up.

"I came in a van, but the van kids are doing horse in the stables," I say.

Again, the girlie boys laugh. "Ride the dark horse!" they say. Together, they make a sick sound. The music keeps changing. The lasers scan the barn like they're searching for a clue. I'm scanning too. No way I'm riding with them.

What is Gordon now? A memory? A missing older stepuncle? My grandmother's boyfriend's brother? I never know how to say it. People put us together. We were a team, even when I didn't want to be. He was a hand down the front of my jogging pants in the bedroom of an abandoned house last summer.

"I see them," I say. In a corner stable, with hay stuck to their faces and arms, the van kids are fucking. It looks as if everyone, somehow, is penetrating everyone else.

Was it August yet? In that abandoned farm house in Pope County? A man becomes a skeleton, gets divided into mismatched parts. He's all wrapped up in the world, and then ripped from it. His skin slips, or is torn off his bones by the jagged chassis of his buddy's vintage El Camino. He gets done in—a hot blade into the fat heart of his small, stupid life.

Someone has flung open the top half of the barn doors. In spirals, in giant breaths, in wide sparkly crests the snow comes, stinging, and suddenly all the people are turning toward it and yelling and covering their eyes and dancing. Now it's like the DJ is playing for the snow, toggling his synthesizer as the gusts fold into the barn. I'm chilled, instantly—a burnt-out filament.

"I'll be outside," I yell to the van kids, who are far off, still penetrating one another, not listening.

Outside people are gathering, trudging like pioneers through the drifts, passing before the electrified snowflakes in the headlights. Is it after midnight? Is it morning? There's someone I know—Gordon, *again?*—dressed like a girl, slamming the car door on a silver Benz, a black feather boa surging between his throat and the wind. "Hello, hello, friend!" he calls. It's not his voice, but it's Gordon's body doddering forward like a bitch, in green high heels. His hands are full. He's holding several glass vials? Test tubes with something living, something fleshy crammed inside each one?

Finally I find the van and stand behind it and let myself throw up.

It was right before he disappeared, I punched Gordon, all awkward, in the neck. I'd aimed for his mouth but missed. "What the hell?" Gordon said to me. "Don't be such a girl. Stand the fuck still." It was sweltering. The sweat stung my scratched mosquito bites. Gordon moved his hand around inside my jogging pants until something happened. "If I have it, you have it too. That's how it works. What's the point of getting tested?" What? Probably nothing. Total anarchy. It was not sexy—that's the last thing—not relief or satisfaction from his greasy hand tugging at me, trying to draw it out and use it to flood the fucking room around us. What else? Like he was trying to drown in it? Like I *deserve* to be left with this, the audacity of a haunting. I get closer to the trees, with the parked cars at my back, and cup some good, clean snow, pack my mouth full and let it melt. I've been thirsty. There's nothing like it. First I was just the sticky clog. That was right after. Now I don't know. My one reasonable desire: thirsty. I'd break-dance all night if I thought I could sweat it out. But then, like, out of nowhere—*damn*, he's so fast. He always was. He's off in the trees. He's running. What is that shit? A giant fucking buck? A ten-pointer? Its antlers all dripping with velvet. He's running after it in his neon heels. "Gordon, dude," I yell to him. "What do you think? I'm going to follow you?"

I pull my hood up. Hot *and* cold. Freezing. Burning. What are they? Opposite thresholds that intersect somewhere in our brains? Two extremes that ultimately cross back into each other? Gordon's like way back in there. He's bending to get some snow too. His hands disappear, up to the elbows. His skirt is so short, showing off his muscular legs. What the fuck is he doing? He's like drilling into the snow. He's making a hole. He's making a place to bury something. A used condom? A wadded-up piece of paper?

All his boring secrets, and mine. *Go figure.*

I just stand there and watch and try to make out what's happening. It's bad though. It's really bad. How can he stand the cold like this? Finally, it's so loud, the deafening burrowing he's doing, and I want to make it stop so I just go to him, dragging my feet through the snow. When I get to him, he shows me what's in the hole and it's hard to see but I'm like, "Holy shit, dude, we really do have to bury this." We dig. We dig until we hit bottom but even then he says it's still not deep enough. I tell him to follow me. We start walking, farther into the frozen woods, searching for a better place. He takes my hand and I let him because it's cold and he seems confused. He has a look on his face, under the fake eyelashes and lipstick, like he's forgotten what he's doing or where he was headed.

"I don't have any friends," I say. "I've never been good at it. I got tested, bro," I lie to him. "I don't have it. Why do you think you're still here, following me?"

"That's a dumb question," he says, lifting up my hand to kiss my cold knuckles. "Does it matter why I'm here, man? I just am." He kisses my hand and wrist several times before letting my arm drop.

Maybe he loves me. It's hard to say. My breath rolls out like exhaust fumes in the freezing air. I spot the buck again, raking his antlers against a small tree. "There it is," I say, hoping to jog Gordon's memory.

"Yes! It's the wrong season for that," Gordon says. "We have to do something." He's upset. He's shaking his head, like maybe it's his fault this is happening.

"Some things just get mixed up," I say. "It's been happening to me a lot. It's not your fault."

"Hell, I know that, dude. If anyone's to blame, it's you. My mother called you. You need to talk to her. She knows. You should just accept that."

Quickly the wind kicks up, dumping snow from the branches. He lets go of my hand and then he's gone. I don't see him anywhere. The buck raises his head up, smelling the air around us. He treads softly into the woods and then he's gone too. I'm alone out here. I don't know where I'm at. There's only the sound of the snow, an infinite amount of crystal particles forming and falling apart for miles in every dark direction.

I've never had to miss anyone I was afraid of. Some days all I wanted to know was where he'd went to. And others . . . I was so fucking cold—all the way down to my bones—expecting him to show back up, to be standing in the kitchen when I got home or walk up behind me in the gas station. But I was also hoping, I can say it now, that he never actually would.

Dioramas

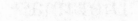

She was washing a dish when she saw the crack. A good plate, one from her mother's black Depression set, like a lightning strike—a fine bolt with tines that randomly forked. Her life was like this, a blunt mistake followed by a series of driftless decisions. Every day, on a faint loop beneath her habits, was the soft dream of a sudden escape.

She enjoyed walking through bean fields and often wandered through the fields beyond the house with her hair teased out like the nest of a large, neurotic bird. The wild construction encircled her petite skull and each time the wind blew, the bangs flapped like a battered wing over her heavily made-up eyes. She wore her stone-washed jeans so tight she could hardly fit a dollar in the pocket, and when she walked she played Cher's nineteenth studio release, *Heart of Stone*, at maximum volume on her Sony Walkman. She'd recently purchased this album on sale at Walmart and found it touched a place so deep inside her it was beyond the grasp of most things in her life. She sang along to every track, and was fond of performing "If I Could Turn Back

Time" a cappella, in the bathroom, so long as the house was empty, such as when the children were at school. It was 1989—The Year of the Snake according to a laminated place mat she'd stolen from China Palace. On her little walks alone she liked to observe: the gray cement of the heavy sky, the anemic farmhouses and the phallic coal silos, the giant grasshoppers that took useless attempts at flight from among the endless bean rows. Occasionally she'd remove her headphones to listen at the insects' alien chatter. Their language struck her as murderous and aroused. She walked nearly every day, always until she came to the same place at the very edge of the woods where someone had abandoned an old, wooden raccoon trap. It was a weathered box with a fall-down trapdoor propped up by a petrified stick. When peering into the trap, Pam witnessed other realities: the silver-lit mouths of caves on unreachable mountainsides, sacred garments sewn from the feathers of prehistoric birds, men with manes of hair expertly braided into hammocks that hung down their mighty backs. Also mansions with glass elevators. Also long sterling earrings like the ones Cher wore on the album cover of *Heart of Stone*. There were even miniature replicas of rooms in the box that Pam had occupied as a young girl. Once she looked inside and saw the child-Pam on her hands and knees, rubbing her bottom against the leg of an antique Pembroke—she had a habit back then of rubbing herself against things, like a dog. She'd been a frail and horny child. Her mother had always made a joke of this to cousins over the phone, as if it proved something—that Pam was untamed? Or developmentally impaired?

How difficult the years had been for Pammy's mommy. Poor Mommy! Often it was implied that Pam was the primary agent of Mommy's fabulous misery. Even Mommy's death, which may or may not have been a suicide, was inevitably pinned on Pam.

Deeper into the shadowy woods, beyond the spot occupied by the little wooden trap, everything remained motionless and quiet.

At home she vacuumed. Or else watched MTV. Or read articles in her women's magazines: "What He Wishes You Were Doing in the Bedroom!" "Vaginas, How Does Yours Compare?" Wouldn't it be nice, she thought, if her husband returned from work to find she had a more perfect vagina, or to surprise him one evening with a new oral skill. She kept her Walkman on while she bleached the toilets. Before mopping she flung a palm-ful of talcum powder into the air and let the cloud waft while she lip-synced "Just Like Jesse James" before the pristine face of the bathroom mirror.

The smell of bleach in the house gave her a reckless feeling. She turned the Walkman off when she heard someone calling her name from another room. Except no one was there. They were all still at work and school. She returned to the bathroom and raised the window in order to partake in one of the secret cigarettes she kept above the medicine chest. Outside, on the ledge, a wasp sat, furiously grooming itself.

It wasn't youth, necessarily, that she coveted as she approached these middle years. She wasn't interested in reentering her vapid, bloodthirsty teenage dreams. But it was something *like* youth—access, maybe, to a world where one's identity remained fluid, and naturally lubricated? A place where the possibilities still burned like barn fires in every direction.

One was not tethered, as a teenager, Pam thought later while vacuuming out the closets. One was expected to transform, almost daily, as a teen.

THE CHILDREN ROLLED in after sundown, sweaty from their after-school activities, calling out for clean underwear and food items that weren't in the house. The stench they carried with them was a musky, hormonal combination of perfumes that made Pam feel affectionate and repelled. She wanted to pay more attention to the children, really, she did. But instead she would yell, "Go build something! Go dream!" in a shrill, dead tone from the La-Z-Boy.

Motherhood was a mysterious hole in a wall she'd entered, wetly, on a stifling evening in 1973, drunk on orange schnapps and too hot to say no to unprotected sex. Of course she had no idea she was saying yes to anything except the darting night-birds, to the beads of sweat gliding down the inverted arch of her spine as her head hung out the car's rear window, to her own hair wrapped around her throat as Richard's massive prick filled her up like a bathtub.

She was just now beginning her exit from that mysterious hole, all these years later, to the sight of expensive furniture dramatically positioned around her living room. She was waking up and her children were growing armpit hair. The whole house, in fact, was growing hairier and hungrier and where had she been exactly? Some outer space? Another distant dimension tucked thin as skin beneath the obvious realm?

The house had become a giant puzzle in which the pieces continued to multiply. She watched TV and made sure all the bills were paid on time. She allowed Janice and Brock and Richard their daily orbits while the unoccupied space of the house diminished, filling with all the discounted items Richard brought home each week. "Very *deep* discounts," he liked to say, punctuated by his smutty wink: Guess jeans by Marciano, seasonal wall art, compact stereos, monogrammed thermoses, crystal carafes, gimmicky exercise equipment, a programmable coffee maker, Calvin Klein underwear, lotions containing rare minerals, her Sony Walkman. Richard was the manager of a large department store and had full access to all items on clearance. Regularly he purchased discount designer suits that he had tailored to fit snugly at the inseam. No surprise most of his employees called him Dick.

And somehow. Just beneath the visible world—that twisted-up other domain into which she slipped so smoothly—may as well have been on the deserted beach of some hazy, subterranean lake, lounging like a drunk with her dead mother.

After the supper dishes were cleared, Pam stared through a breach in the drapes, observing the manner in which darkness obscured the textures of the lawn. Cher was everywhere—a flickering hologram. In the diseased rose hedge. In the even carpet of the grass. In the ditch by the road where the weeds grew high enough to hide a body. Behind her, even, in the living room, Cher lay spread-eagle on the sofa. Just as she began to feel herself flush at the thought, maybe even become a little turned-on, the porch light of the farmhouse across the road came on, illuminating two terra-cotta buffalo heads on each side of the huge front door. Each pot contained a single erotically shaped cactus. They had not been there the day before. The giant farmhouse had been on the market since 1985. No one came to view it anymore. The cross-eyed widow that owned it did her giddy disclosure too many times, saying, "There's a dozen underground rivers beneath here. Old coal land! All the mine shafts flood every time it rains! What the coal company ought to do is buy up the place, pay me a bucket of money and let the mutated fish take it over." The coal company had actually made an offer to Richard and Pam. They'd turned it down, holding out for more money, same as the widow. They were the last two remaining residents out this far.

Pam could see the front door was freshly painted: a creamy, pale shade of orange. It was a full-on renovation. The door's three clear windows had been replaced with frosted blue panes. Obviously the new owners were trying to compensate for something.

Richard summoned Pam into the bathroom, requesting another can of beer be brought to him in the shower. She didn't begrudge him. She smoked in there, using the drain as an ashtray.

IN THE MORNING, after the school bus pulled away, Richard brought out the vibrator. He liked to watch her use it on herself while he shoved his prick so aggressively down her throat it brought tears to her eyes. Why they did this *after* making the bed was anyone's guess. The bedroom possessed a stagey neatness that contradicted their rough sex. Or brandished it? As was the case in the more tastefully produced pornos Richard brought back from Video Emporium. In these films women were typically splayed across pink satin bedspreads, bent over wicker ottomans in beachfront town houses void of all personal effects. Occasionally Richard would pull her hair while attempting to control the vibrator himself. He was not graceful. He longed to execute too many fantasies at once. His hands were impatient. She was never excited by the arrangement, but complied because, truly, it meant so much to him. She could see the gratitude twisting like a summer storm in his tired eyes. He badly wanted to be a manly aggressor. His hostility lacked hunger though. She *knew* what hunger looked like. And his was a bad reenactment of it. Afterward he pulled her gently to the edge of the bed and continued getting at her, softer now, with the blue toy, until she signaled she'd climaxed too. It was shaped like a dolphin, the toy, and her body lapped rhythmically against the deep diving while Richard whispered "You're beautiful" and "I love you."

Regrettably, this was nothing like the celebrity role-playing scenarios she described to him after a few drinks on the patio.

He washed up in the bathroom and with a bottle in each hand misted a veil of cologne that he walked determinedly through, right out the front door, leaving behind the doomed smells of Aramis and Drakkar Noir.

She stood perfectly still at the mouth of the hall, feeling as if she were about to be delivered from the belly of the house. A small pressure could be felt. The whole place was dead quiet. The plastic flower arrangements in their fluted vases were dusty, and she could still smell the base notes of Richard's cologne. She was thinking of that distant, dusk-lit era right before puberty engulfed her. She'd had a fantasy back then of being a DMV employee: the aseptic office, the cryptic vision-screening machine, the ladies' glasses dangling from gold, rococo chains. A girl's life could be filled with moments like this: longings for positions of power and beauty.

The years had passed in crooked, hurtful ways, stranding her like a bored time traveler with Richard and the children.

She decided she'd replace the fake flowers with something more interesting, feathers or shards of broken glass. But not before her walk. She surveyed the neighbor's house again. Two shirtless hunks were spreading red pebbles down the driveway, like icing on a giant cake, while another, dopier man finagled a leather sectional through the pretentious front door.

She put on her headphones and wandered through the green fields that skirted the sun-flecked woods. The trapdoor, propped up by its stick, made a little awning for the box. Outside, it was black with decay and dappled neon with moss. It was a lovely thing, and more alive today. When she knelt down, hunching a little to clear the awning, she observed a quivering cone of fire. Below the orange fire was a city with spires and slender onyx skyscrapers. At the edge of the city was a steel mill—the same steel mill that had stood like a demon empire at the end of the road she'd grown up on. It was a tangled gathering of scaffolds and pipes that broke through a copper skyline, filling the air around with a bitter smell, like old blood. The version in the box was small enough to fit in her palms. She did not reach out. She leaned in closer to admire it. Her head cast a shadow, throwing the scene into darkness, causing a hundred little lights to blink on at once—the lights defined the shape of every building. There were violent raspings and dense billows of steam no bigger than cotton balls, all of it lit by the glow of the constantly churning flame, dripping like a cracked-open sun over the busy diorama. Near the back she noticed a cluster of sow bugs crawling across the roof of a smaller building. How did she miss this? Lonely and darkened at the edge of a tar-paved road was her very own girlhood home. Every red shingle, every painted-shut window, her own mother even, in her strapless romper, sitting on the lopsided porch, drinking Miller High Life from a microscopic wineglass. A crow the size of a housefly perched atop a thread-thin power line, and a cat in the lot next door stared up suspiciously from a canopy of folded-over weeds. Pam watched for a long time, mesmerized by the delicate movements of the weeds and the bird and her doll-like mother, even the way the light from the burning pyramid in the sky reflected in the little wineglass each time her mother raised it to take a drink. She observed her mother going in and out of the house, tugging at her revealing romper, refilling the glass, until finally the mini-mother walked down the steps and fell down drunk on the lawn, exposing herself to anyone passing by. Pammy knelt and listened to her mother's piggish snore. She expected her tiny daddy to come out and carry Mommy inside. But he never did.

Pam backed away from the box to stretch a crick in her neck, causing the little safety lights of the mill to flick off. There was a quick hiss of steam and the cone of fire diminished into a willowy pipe. The whole mill contracted abruptly into itself, like a crude mechanical toy, leaving behind the smell of rust and chlorinated water.

AT HOME SHE lay about in the recliner watching *Top 20 Video Countdown* on the jumbo TV. She awoke to the racket of night insects in the flower beds, and her daughter, Janice, saying, "Wake up, Mother. Meet the new neighbor!" Janice and the neighbor girl stood in front of the TV: two silhouettes examining each other's Swatches before a George Michael video on mute.

"Excuse me?" Pam said, reaching for the lamp. The neighbor girl stood before her in the buttery light, wearing a pink Mickey Mouse T-shirt that stopped directly below the girl's perfect breasts.

"Hello, Janice's mother," the girl said in a flippant, adult voice.

"We want the television," Janice said.

The girl's jeans were high and tight, like a designer bandage. Between the T-shirt and denim her skin showed, smooth and tan as a suede coat. The TV flicked between commercials. Somewhere a cat screamed in heat. Pam felt trapped. She'd removed her pants before falling asleep and had nothing on beneath the afghan. "Tia just moved here from New Mexico," Janice said. "She came over to roll up your car windows. Isn't that nice? It's about to storm."

Pam turned to look out the window. The night was starry and still.

"Honestly, it could change in an instant," Tia said. "I spotted a strange cloud earlier. Cumulus, or possibly cumulonimbus. It contained a shadow." She said this dryly, seating herself on the arm of the sofa, gesturing at the window with a bony finger. Her pupils were large, and luminous as varnish, and her lashes grew forth hectically like those of a beautiful horse.

"How did you get here, again?" Pam said.

"We bought the farmhouse across from you," Tia said, rising to adjust Pam's blanket, politely concealing a nude thigh. "But I walked over."

"From Mexico?"

Tia laughed, a bright, orbital laugh that caused Pam to laugh too. "From New Mexico, I flew!" she said.

Pam was not entirely conscious, she realized.

Janice looked to be in agony. She hauled Tia out of the room. "Please put some pants on, Mother. We're coming back to watch a video in here."

The girls returned with several empty onion bags. They cut them apart and sewed them back together again with dental floss. In the end they had two matching pairs of mesh gloves.

"Make me ralph. What a skeezer," Janice said, referring to a girl from school. "He's a scum. Gross me out," she said about the handicapped boy up the road.

Tia held out her newly gloved hands. "Tell me about the preps and jocks," she said, leaning into Janice, angling to inhale deeply from her hair. She appeared pleased by the scent, smiling intensely at Pam as she took another deep breath. The girl's grin revealed a gold-capped canine. The tooth was shocking. Her teeth were otherwise orderly inside her stunning mouth, but the dental work was wrong. The tooth pointed down sharply, like a shiny metal fang.

The teen language was exhausting. Janice sounded like a bad actress—a young woman practicing to be a grown bitch. Tia sipped her Diet Coke and thoughtfully observed Debbie Gibson's live performance of "Electric Youth." Debbie was wearing an off-the-shoulder lace top.

"I find that so sexy!" Pam said.

"So do I!" Tia said, as if grateful to Pam for mentioning it.

"Mother! Go away!" Janice squalled.

"And don't you just love all those little belts?" Tia continued, employing again her buoyant adult tone.

"So what do your parents do, Tia?" Pam asked.

Tia tapped her upper lip and sighed. "Mostly? They travel in Europe and Asia."

Pam waited before realizing this was all the girl was offering. "Why is that, exactly?" she asked.

"The lecture circuit," she said. "Native American culture and history. The atrocities! Other countries seem to have a greater interest in the modern Indian. Less guilt, Daddy always says. Plus they love judging the failures of Americans."

"Don't we all?" Pam said, not entirely certain what she meant.

It was cut off, Tia's Mickey Mouse T-shirt—with dull scissors it looked like. When the girl reached for her soda, Pam could see the slick undercurve of her tiny brown tits.

Richard came home from work with a mustache. Pam squirmed at the sight of it. It had a severe effect on his face. The

TV-detective look, the greasy porn star of it. This, and the dramatic tailoring of his pants, was a too-obvious metaphor for the pervert that lurked below Richard's funny face.

"You look like a skeezer," Pam said.

"A skeezer? Is that a scum?" he asked.

Brock, their son, entered too. The whole family had swarmed like sharks to a bait bucket. "What the hell? Is this family hour?" Brock asked. He stared arrogantly. "I'm hungry," he announced, looking at Tia. His voice pitched down abruptly, like a cassette tape played too many times.

"Take a picture," Janice called to him, "because that's all you're going to get."

"I would," Brock said, "if my camera wasn't so fucking hard right now." With this he fondled at his crotch through the loose folds of his fluorescent parachute pants.

"Son!" Richard said, in a tone of scolding alarm and pride.

"This is too much," Pam said.

"You're a scum, Brock!" Janice said.

Tia lifted her hair off her shoulders, flinging it gently back so that it fell again around her face like a rippling curtain.

"Tia, honey?" Pam said. "Did you happen to see that recent television interview with Cher, the one where she discussed the struggles of her biracial heritage? I've often wondered if she's an icon in your community?"

"Oh, hell," Brock muttered.

"Mother, stop!" Janice said.

"Doesn't she have the bravest outlook on life?" Tia said, with a sincerity that reordered the sharp pitch hanging over the room.

"She's Armenian, though, right? My dad always said Cher has about as much Cherokee in her as a box of dirt from our backyard. Which isn't much, because we lived in New Mexico. It's mostly Apache and Pueblo. Maybe around here there'd be more? Except they're mainly a southern tribe. You're a fan? Of Cher?"

"I am," Pam said. "She had a whole song about it! About being trapped in both worlds, between her Cherokee and white heritage? Was she lying?" Pam's voice broke. Her hands were shaking, her forehead suddenly clammy. Out of nowhere she found herself desperate for someone's approval. It was a feeling she'd been missing in her life for far too long.

"TWO WORDS," RICHARD later said, after Tia left, "illegal immigrant. From Mexico. Most likely a prostitute."

"Wouldn't you just love that," Pam said. "And that was more than two words."

Janice hid her face in the decorative sofa pillows, her shoddy gloves already falling apart across her palms. Tia had abandoned hers between the cushions. "Her family moved here from the rez in New Mexico, Daddy!"

"More like Old Mexico!" Richard said.

After everyone was asleep, Pam went back into the living room to search for Tia's gloves. She dug them from the sofa and slipped them on. She was delighted to find they were a perfect fit.

THE GIRL'S HAIR was as lustrous and dark as used motor oil. It flung off a suggestive sheen each time she turned her head.

Pam wanted hair like that. She drifted unevenly, limply, back to the nights she had played the 45 of Cher's "Half-Breed" in her bedroom as if it were the soundtrack to another, imaginary life. It hurt to hear someone call Cher a liar. But maybe, for all these years, Pam had taken the song too seriously?

During her afternoon nap, Pam dreamed of wearing Tia's hair around like a wig. Attempting to explain this to Richard over dinner, she realized her dream implied a traditional scalping.

She recalled hearing of a case in high school, back in Indiana, of a Cuban girl who'd claimed to be Native American in an attempt to avoid deportation. What ever had happened to that girl? Pam hoped she'd married, and was still in the country, living out some titillating American dream.

PAM OBSERVED TIA waiting for the bus. She was perched on the freshly massacred stump of an ancient elm that had been sawed from the yard the afternoon before. Not a very Pueblo thing to do, Pam thought. Ritually, dumbly, Pam had stared across the street into its woven branches for over a decade, admiring its peacefully bowed head of tear-shaped leaves. Now the girl sat on the smooth pedestal of its corpse, organizing her backpack and teasing her bangs with a pink comb until the hair looked like ruffled plumage. Tia blasted the bangs with hair spray, then tucked the massive can into her purse. Pam could not make out the label, but was curious as to which brand was being used.

The front door was the ugliest affair. In the upstairs window, an enormous fuchsia dream catcher swung back and forth in perfect measures like a pendulum on its string. Perhaps a ceiling fan was on?

"YOU'RE LOSING IT, Mother," Janice said, surprising Pam during an impromptu buffalo dance she was attempting in the kitchen. Pam turned the Walkman down and smiled, careful not to reveal any embarrassment, lest her daughter think she was ashamed of private joy.

During the most transcendent part of her dance Pam had encountered a muscular shaman with a crown of braided hair that extended into tightly laced pigtails across his glistening chest. Beside a yellow fire inside a grass-covered wigwam, he'd presented Pam with a sacred agate and turquoise belt so heavy and complicated her arms still ached with the thought of its power. They'd walked along a dirt path that Pam assumed was the Trail of Tears. Miles they traveled, until they'd arrived in her own backyard near the tree line of the woods. Her recliner was there, waiting for her like a cheap throne beside the trap.

"I FEEL DEBBIE Gibson has too small of a face," Pam said to Janice. "I wonder how I'd look as a blond?"

"No," Janice said. "You'd look like shit. You're more of a *Cher* anyway." This was in no way a compliment, and it injured Pam. Janice didn't appreciate Cher. She didn't understand the brazen bewitchment—Cher's ability to conjure rolling fog and animal power and black leather, to stroke with her voice the tired heart like a shy hostage about to be set free.

To be fair, Pam mostly pretended to appreciate the children. It wasn't something she was proud of. When she was visibly overwhelmed, Richard would say, "Kids are people too, Pammy. They just want to know you're on their side." But Pam wasn't so sure. Most *people* she knew didn't stomp out of supermarkets when they couldn't purchase the expensive shampoo. Kids were always demanding more. Sneaking all the chips and dip before Pam got any herself. She badly desired a thing spared of their animal greed.

AFTER LYING AROUND all afternoon on account of a head-ache, Pam hid in the bathroom, enjoying one of her secret cigarettes, blowing smoke into the exhaust. She had to shade her eyes even inside the house. Her allergies were severe and there was a whine like a distress signal happening in her inner ear. Janice had sliced her thumb on the new shards of glass Pam installed in the vases around the dining area—fat, brutal-looking pieces procured from a crate of broken frames that had once contained the children's most asinine school photos. The effect of these glass bouquets was that of frozen crystal fires. Pam was entranced. Her daughter's dramatic whining, and the gross gash, sent everyone running. Brock was holed up in his room with the door locked, blaring Run-D.M.C., ignoring all requests to lower the volume. After a couple of drags Pam extinguished the ciga-rette into an empty beer can Richard had left on the soap tray. Outside, in the drive, Richard was screwing on his new license plates. Pam could see him through the bathroom window. His sneakers were as white as the clouds above the bean fields—whiter, even. His new license plate, she could see, said 2THEMAX. He'd already fastened hers on. 3THEMAX, it said.

Richard really could be such a dick.

She snuck out the back door. The bean plants flicked their fuzzy leaves. Through the noise-canceling headphones Cher sang about wishing for a heart of stone. Pam did wish this, frequently. The drumbeat was a hand smacking a paper bag. Cher's voice trembled like hot rubber. The sunlit stage of the trap sat neatly along the viny edge of the woods. Pam's pulse roared. The kudzu tangled. At the back of the box, curled in a corner, was a tiny hairless donkey. Its skin was blue, nearly transparent, slick and shiny as plastic wrap. She could have counted each bone in the cage of its ribs. The donkey was no bigger than a fist. She was sure it was dead. Always there had been a certainty that whatever appeared in the box arrived through a weak slit in reality, like a wound that had rotted through to the invisible world. This emaciated, bald animal, though, could have walked from somewhere. It could have gone inside for shelter and died. It had to be the tiniest donkey ever—with darling, folded ears, a ropy tail, stunted horse head, and the most unsettling part, a long, kinky head of hair, just like Cher. Just as Pam thought she would reach in and scoop it up, its frail hindquarters twitched in a hypnic jerk. It took a spasmed breath. His bony chest rose, and a whistled rasp escaped his wet nostrils, the breath jostling the gorgeous curly locks that fell before its face. The precious little ass was alive and dreaming. She had never put her hands in the box. It was a decision she'd made at the beginning. The contents were untouchable. She feared the consequences, despite any desire to interact. Before she could touch it though, the thin-skinned little ass brayed, causing a chartreuse ball of fire to pop from its lanky mouth. The donkey blinked at the fireball, then brayed again, releasing a second, bigger blaze that rushed forth, blackening the wall of the box before bouncing off in an audible backdraft that engulfed the shivering creature, burning the baby to a crisp, leaving only its charred skeleton wrapped in steaming skin. The whole abrupt scene was made even more terrible by the goofy horror of the donkey's two teeth jutting from its scorched jaw. Somehow the wig was unharmed, plopped crookedly atop the sizzling bag of bones.

She ran home. The grasshoppers popped around her ankles like a hundred booby traps. She could still hear Cher rattling from the headphones as she opened the front door. The whole family was there, drooling nearly, over Tia, whose arms were flailing in what appeared to be the dramatic telling of a story. She was on the arm of the sofa again, smiling like a stripper with those bangs like hands clawing at something just above her head. Richard was sitting at the end of the sofa too, with Tia's tiny bare feet resting neatly on his thigh. Tia rushed to Pam. "There you are," she said, "finally!" She embraced Pam so freely, Pam thought she'd never been held like this by anyone. It was the affection of someone who valued her. "Look what I made you!" Tia said, pulling from the pocket of her pleated shorts a pair of earrings. Within the huge hoops were two black-and-white photos of Cher, held in place by red string woven in crisscrosses, suspending Cher's face and body in skimpy crimson webs. "I worked on them all night because I just couldn't stop thinking of what you'd said, about Cher being trapped between the old traditions of her ancestors and the whitewashed world of pop culture." Had Pam said this? She wanted to have said this. She could feel the teardrops ruining her expensive mascara.

"Oh, honey," she said, "I love them."

"I just worry about you!" Tia said, holding the earrings up to Pam's face. "In one of Daddy's best talks, he says the Europeans were terrified of the Natives. Isn't that crazy? I hope you're not scared of me! He says it wasn't because they thought we'd eat their eyeballs or build tipis from their bones. But because they thought we were smarter than them. They couldn't understand why we weren't obsessed with wealth. We could run, we could climb trees, we watched the sky for symbols of things to come, and we didn't need to go out and conquer anything. Being civilized, to the white man, meant working until you owned everything you could see. Being civilized, to the Indian, meant not beating your horse to death when it got too old to be useful. They were terrified we had it right and they'd traveled all this way for the wrong reasons. So we had to be extinguished. I hope you don't mind me saying that."

Pam realized Tia was holding her hand, gripping it tightly. The family sat on the sofa, fidgety and stunned. From across the room, Richard's crotch appeared swollen and alive. Tia stopped speaking but the sound of her voice hung in the air like the last echoes of a bell that had been ringing for an incredibly long time. Pam hoped Richard and the kids weren't too jealous of the attention she was getting.

Pam spent a long time viewing herself in the mirror. The

jewelry transformed her, lying neatly in the ratted nest of her hair, cradling her face like a small, pale egg.

The earrings brought back a memory of her mother screaming into the telephone. Her mother had torn the phone from the wall but was drunk and failed to realize how knotted she was in the cord. Her eyes were wasted cuts in her bloated face. The cord twisted inside an earring, tearing it from the lobe, flicking bloody droplets onto the wall and Pam, in her footed pajamas. After the blood dried, it gave the impression of little brown polka dots. How could she have forgotten the look Mother gave her, like Pam had caused the whole thing? "Go and wash it off, for God sakes! You look like you just killed something!"

Mother's booze-ravaged face was so often contorted into a generator of enduring shame.

EVERYWHERE SHE LOOKED she could see the finest pricks of light like aspirated paint drifting across the horizon— the slow burn of another allergy headache, or maybe just the world quietly disassembling.

Janice and Tia were affixed to each other. They were mining each other's depths. It wasn't hard to do—they were still young and shallow enough to hit bottom. The world was made for teenage girls. Those tiny bodies. Those tiny tits. Early in the morning, at the end of the drive, doing jumping jacks in their leggings and scrunch socks, Janice and Tia were packed into their bodies. They were still in their unripe stages, on the cusp of revealing to the world their hidden meanings. Everywhere, Pam thought, men were waiting to explore them like unreachable caves, while she was left feeling like a condemned flophouse a cop might suspiciously shine a spotlight on in the dark.

"Janice is so strong, isn't she, Pamela?" Tia said, annihilating a slice of the cherry pie she'd baked and brought to the family that afternoon.

"Shouldn't we have baked for you?" Janice said.

"Since when do you bake anything?" Pam asked.

"I would, for Tia!" Janice whined. "Tia is the only one who gets me," she said, shoveling in the pie, turning her nose up at Pam.

"Oh, Janice," Tia said, extending the hand that wasn't destroying the dessert. The girls locked arms and kissed each other primly on the cheek.

"How do I look in these jeans?" Pam asked. "They're Guess! Do they flatter me?"

"Your ass looks like a sack of russet potatoes," Janice said, her mouth half-full.

"Janice, sweetheart!" Tia said, tenderly chiding her. "Elegance, please."

"Sorry," Janice said to Tia. "Forgive me, Mommy," she said to Pam.

"Tia, may I ask what brand of hair spray you use?" Pam asked.

Janice frowned.

Brock rolled his eyes from across the room. "Whores," he said.

"Scum!" Pam said.

"I'm leaving," Brock said.

"Listen, everyone, please. Close your eyes. All of you," Tia said, affectionately stroking the black assembly of leather cords around her tenuous throat. "Listen to the wind. Can't you hear it?"

They listened, or Pam did, at least—as if it weren't there before and suddenly it was. She knew this was only because she hadn't been paying attention. It rustled the trees, clattered a distant chime, pushed small dry things across the concrete patio.

"Let's all have a family night!" Tia said, clasping her hands together.

Pam was only ever good at making plans and then pretending to be upset when she broke them. This was how she knew she was a decent mother—the attempts.

"I'm going to the community center," Brock said. "It's my night."

Brock and his friends had turntables. The sounds they made were shocking. It filled Pam up, briefly.

"Let's crimp each other's hair in my bedroom," Janice said to Tia.

"I'll come too!" Pam said.

"I seriously doubt it, Mother," Janice said.

"Are you doing any new remixes?" Pam asked Brock.

"Fuck off, Mother," Brock said.

"Brock is working on his own original tracks," Tia said. "Aren't you, Brock?"

"Maybe," he said. "Nothing's for sure."

"Go then! I give both of my children over to the world. I set you free!" Pam said.

"Oh, family," Tia said, "I want to heal you."

Pam waited for the children to execute their typical disgust, but they only sat there in silence, relishing the pie, waiting, it seemed, for Tia to follow through. Pam thought she should be furious, but instead she continued studying the dark wreath of necklaces, wondering where Tia had acquired them.

Pam spent the rest of the day eating gummy bears, listening again for the voice of the wind, hoping to hear something crucial. It was hard to hear anything though, over her relentless chewing and the girls' melodious laughter and Brock's record player, which seemed to be going in reverse as he ominously accompanied on an old keyboard he brought down from the attic after deciding to stay in. There was Richard too, counting irately and breathlessly as he jumped rope like a maniac on the front lawn.

"WE NEED TO go out shopping," Pam said to Richard, sliding her fingers into the mesh gloves. "There are many new things I'm longing for. I'm desperate for a new look, something fresh."

"You spend too much time alone," Richard said.

"I stay occupied," she said, thinking fondly of the trees and the kind box.

"Tia's been telling the children you need help."

"Help with what? The dishes? Isn't that sweet of her. She seems very engaged with what's going on around her."

"No, Pam. Like, mental help. This might prove her point. The children and I don't necessarily disagree. You could talk to someone again. What about Charlie? You loved Charlie. He really seemed to help after Daddy passed."

"Charlie was a dirty old man! I couldn't stand him. It was Linda I loved."

"I thought he helped you. You seemed better after those talks."

"He helped me out of my clothes once while he had me under deep hypnosis! That's about it."

"That never happened, Pam. Please don't."

"What is this? A witch hunt? What happened to Tia, the Mexican prostitute? Suddenly she's a mental health professional *and* a spiritual guru?"

"What about that listening-to-the-wind stuff? You said that was nice."

"You should put this on," she said, tossing him a baseball cap.

Richard looked confused. Suddenly he was claiming he only wanted to be himself in the bedroom. She didn't buy it. He wasn't himself even out of the bedroom. Who was he anyway? And why wouldn't he be Marky Mark for an evening, and she Debbie Gibson? Last time she'd allowed him to choose! That was ages ago. She was Alyssa Milano and he was the R & B sensation Luther Vandross. When Richard was Luther, he said things like "Rock my world, lover girl," and "Do it to me, teen queen. Yes, yes, ivory princess!" It hadn't worked. Richard's Luther was a joke. And he would never pick a specific member of New Kids on the Block. When asked to take turns being all of them, in the manner of a classic gang bang, Richard had gone limp in her hands. Possibly her desires were too interior for him to fathom.

"New Kids on the Block would be so jealous, Marky Mark!" she said, pleading. "They could only dream of conquering this electric, youthful body!" She went on like this until he conceded. He put on his Calvin Klein underwear and the baseball cap. Pam situated the wig on her head—a ratty, blond shag from the Halloween trunk. "Can you hear all those fans chanting outside the walls of our mansion?" Pam asked. "They're cheering for us!"

Richard was posing aggressively at the foot of the bed. "Yeah," he said. "Now see if you can't drown out their screams with the sound of your sucking."

"All those young girls out there," Pam whispered, stretching out the neck of her nightshirt to expose a shoulder. "They only wish they were me!" She was crawling toward him on all fours across the mattress. "They wanna wear my skin like a bodysuit."

"Is that so?" Richard said, staring down at her, erect and dismal.

Afterward, swapping out their sweaty pillowcases, Pam said, "Love's wings are broken too soon, Richard." This was a Cher song. It made Pam feel good, to pull these flaming symbols from the air and expound them, daringly, like Cher. "You think you'll knock me off my feet until I'm flat on the floor? Until my heart is crying Indian and I'm begging for more? Come on, baby! Show me what that loaded gun is for! I'm gonna shoot you down, Jesse James."

"Whatever you want, Pammy," Richard said, turning to face the wall.

She lay her head down next to his, feeling dizzy. It was sexy, and exalting, being someone else. She only wished he thought so too. She pressed her palms against her temples, making the fingertips touch over her eyes like a pliant steeple.

THE ANGRY FIRE had blasted above the asymmetry of the mysterious configurations of the steel mill, where she'd grown up. In that forgotten part of town one wasn't inclined to walk the streets after dark. Every week while her father played his music in the basement, her mother toppled down the steps and slept like a homeless person on the lawn. How luxurious, Pam thought, to indulge in one's bad ideas until you disintegrated back into molecules, drifted again through the lucent atmosphere like an isolated shower of black blood, heading nowhere.

The things Pam had the longest were the things she loved the most. Her yellow oven mitts. Her stainless steel ice bucket. Her 45 of "Half-Breed." The garbage disposal, for some reason. She loved how it whirred like a little helicopter taking in a bowl of old food, mutilating leftovers into the plumbing. Where did they go? What happened to them after they got there? When the children were smaller they would run from the bus and into the woods behind the house. They'd run until they fell down in the leaf piles. This was how she'd discovered the box. It was just sitting there. Waiting for her. The children would dig toadstools from the undergrowth and hide them in their pockets. She'd find the flattened mushrooms days later while sorting the laundry. She would allow the kids to burn the piles of leaves in the yard, sending out smoke signals over the neighborhood. What other mother allowed her children to play with fire? With the cracked half of an old kiddie pool, they'd fan the smoke. "Don't get too close!" she'd call from behind a magazine. Back then, she only had to say it once.

It wasn't too many years later, they had taken the children to Garden of the Gods Wilderness and Wildlife Refuge. The massive, rust-colored bluffs jutted over a forest just beginning to bud. The children hurried past the sights, both of them listless and overdressed. She and Richard were on a narrow path, wedged between the million-year-old rock formations, when he turned to her. "Are we Menudo or New Kids on the Block?" he'd asked.

"NKOTB, all the way," she'd said.

They kissed hard, and stretched all around, for miles, the tree limbs were bare and pocked with tiny green sprouts. To be young, she had thought, and in love. And now, to be neither.

"YOU'VE GOT TO dry up, Mother!" her father always said. Her mother hated this. "I'm already dry as a bone, Bill. Take me out of the fire. I'm done!" Pam understood even then that it was meant to be ironic, when they found Mother's bloated body in the bathtub, the beer cans precisely lined along the ledge. The steel mill had been shut down, not long after, and Mother was being lobbed like a rocket toward the deepest quadrants of eternity. Pam wondered how long it took to get there—centuries, perhaps, spent burning off the fuel of one's dumbest dreams until you reached the center of forever.

On the day Mother was removed from the house, Daddy had rolled cigarettes on the porch. "You hungry?" he'd said. He worked the tobacco into a tube. Pam studied his thumbs, the way they deftly spun the fragile paper.

"No, I'm not," she'd lied.

"I did it for you," he'd said. "It was basically your idea." Had he meant pressuring Mommy to dry up, or drowning her? She hadn't asked. Did it matter? Mother would have boozed herself to death all on her own. But perhaps it was a kindness, on both their parts? Either way, they were in it together now. Behind them on the porch, dozens of Japanese beetles swarmed the windows, the sound of their hard bodies hitting the screen like the ticking of a sad clock.

SHE WALKED DOWN the drive to get the mail before heading through the harvested field to commune with the box. In the center of the open trap the tiny flame was back, spraying down like an inverted fountain. She would burn that outrageously, she thought, someday. She would conquer, like this assertive fire. Or she would stand at the end of the driveway wearing all of her turquoise bracelets at once, holding her utility bills, watching the crazed squirrels scatter across the lip of the gutters. Her past had come to meet her. She had been leashed like a dog to her parents' worst deeds, smelted from their blackest shit. Without even meaning to, she'd taken up the torch of all their pointless traditions.

The windows on the neighbor's front door were like little blue lockets she wanted to crack open. Inside, the neighbors were probably smoking their peace pipes. She'd never seen the parents, but surely they were in there doing Native American things. The dream catcher still swung in the window. And the rest—what she couldn't see—she could feel: Arrowheads being sharpened. The spirits of wild animals worshipped. Immense blankets woven from the hair of their ancestors. They were in there singing about the buffalo, the quail, the bald eagle. They were breathing one another's sweet, wise breaths back and forth between them. Pam stood, trapped in the heat of every possibility, and then a movement, a shadow inside the locket, and the giant castle door opening up.

Tia stepped out—sashayed, really—wearing a massive feather headdress nearly twice the size of her head. It had two raccoon tails that hung down either side of her tan face. Pam caught a glimpse inside the huge house before Tia slammed the door. It was nearly empty, the walls blank, only the extravagant leather sofa sat in the center of the otherwise vacant room. Tia's crown of white and red feathers stabbed out like shiny spears. She went over and mounted the stump, raised her hands above her head, ran her fingers back and forth through the air as if gathering it up. She cupped her hands and brought them to her mouth, taking in a huge breath, then blowing it back out slowly in every direction, as if putting out some invisible fire all around her.

Finally she acknowledged Pam standing alone in the field. Tia bowed gracefully, holding on to the headdress to keep it from toppling. She dismounted the stump and walked over. "This was my father's headdress," she called from across the road. "It's vintage! Basically a sacred artifact."

Up close it looked cheap and ragged, like an old gas station tchotchke. Pam reached out to pet one of the tails. The two women stood watching each other calmly. A hard breeze surfaced, disturbing the feathers, beating the raccoon tails against Tia's cheeks, flipping Pam's huge hair too, like a stiff weed.

"I'd like to show you something," Pam said, immediately surprised she'd said it.

"I thought you'd never ask," Tia said, flinging the shabby feathers off her forehead.

They were almost to the edge of the woods when Tia stopped. "Life happens to be the sum of many small, barely conscious decisions," she said. "You should keep that in mind, moving forward."

"Don't I know it!" Pam replied. "But why, is the real question?"

Tia stood militantly, her head craned to observe the many cardinals flicking erratically among the highest branches. She walked directly up to the little box and, with all her strength, shoved it backward a few feet toward the trees.

"What are you doing?" Pam cried out, except the box had produced an earsplitting squeal, like the sound of many metal gears grinding beneath the earth. The trap was attached to something. Pam could feel the mechanism rumbling below her feet. As it rolled through the leaves and dirt, the wooden walls of the box folded down until it was completely flattened out, making a perfect platform in front of a small hole where the trap had always sat. The two women stood over the opening in awe, peering down.

"How did you know?" Pam asked, her entire body throbbing.

"It was a hunch," Tia said. "Obviously the box was put there to hide something. Like most inconspicuous things."

"My God," Pam said, moving into a better position, allowing the sun to illuminate the dark cavern below.

"It's enormous down there. It must be an old mine shaft," Tia said. "Down where all those old Indian bones transform into coal. Shall we go in?"

"Down inside?" asked Pam.

"Don't you want to?" asked Tia.

Tia put her hands on Pam's shoulders and pulled her away from the hole. Tia lifted a muscular leg and stomped around the opening. Stones and the earth tumbled down, clacking musically at the faraway bottom, echoing after they hit.

"You'll fit perfectly now," Tia said.

"Is this it?" Pam said. "Are we really doing this?"

"I just figure friends should help friends, Pam. Woman to woman. You know?"

"Are we friends?" Pam asked.

"Of course! More than friends, I'd say." Tia patted Pam gently on the back.

Pam wasn't sure. A faint trickling of water could be heard inside the cave. The underground magnified it, causing even the dripping to take on an infinite quality.

Tia knelt down. "Hello!" she called. The cave caught her voice and held it for a moment before flinging it in a dozen directions.

"Time is different down there," Pam said.

"Undoubtedly," Tia said, taking Pam's hand. "You first?"

There was a rocky ledge right below the platform of the trap, and other stones like steps that led into the blackness, making the descent seem irresistible.

Pam had her Walkman. She put it on after finding the first landing. Cher's voice scored the dank air so finely it was as if she were down there with Pam, singing to her from inside a thousand moist hallways. There was the silver light in the distance, mirrored by the glistening deposits of coal that ran in bent seams through every corridor.

After a minute, Pam swore she heard her mother's slurred, raspy alto, attempting to harmonize with Cher. She picked the most obvious hallway and stepped inside. Maybe Tia had come to help her after all, she thought. Pam felt different, smaller. The hallway she'd chosen widened into another, larger cavern. There was a placid pool at her feet where dangerous fish darted in the murk, disturbing the sparkling sediment. Reflected in the water she could see a fire, and an ugly shaman behind her, descending in a glass elevator. She didn't even notice when Tia slid the box back, hiding the opening again. She could hardly hear the elaborate gears grinding overhead, their rusty teeth firmly catching as the trap locked into place.

Acknowledgments

So many people helped to make this book. Over a decade of my life went in to these stories. But I wasn't alone. I was helped by the wisdom and work of numerous lovely and smart people: friends, family, colleagues, teachers, editors and one unwaveringly thoughtful agent. I don't even know where to begin except the beginning. Through every version of every story my precious friend, Melissa Borries, the poet laureate of my heart, has given me endless amounts of supernatural insight and encouragement. There wouldn't be a book without her. Also, Amy Baily, whose rare combination of genius and kindness helped me to write beyond myself. And, of course, my first creative writing teacher, Joey Flamm-Costello.

The world would be impenetrably dark without my friends and I have been lucky to have the kind who have always been gracious when I needed help: Gina Bayless, Lizz Cooley, Jona Whipple, Julai Whipple, Melanie Lentz, Robert Devillez, Kyle Winkler, Heather Overby, Maurine Ogbaa, Amanda Goldblatt, Katya

Apekina and Trevor Wood. I am also grateful for my invaluable teachers: Rodney Jones, Beth Lordan, Kathryn Davis, Mike Magnuson, Marshall Klimasewiski and Kelly Wells.

I'm forever grateful for the love and support of my family: Carol Brooks, Paula France, John Mark Dennis, Lucy and Delaney Dennis, Shawn Owen and my sister and best friend, Monica Dennis.

Thank you so much to John Freeman, Ellah Allfrey, Patrick Ryan and Claire Boyle. And especially to PJ Mark and Mark Doten for their patience and generosity and for making me feel so deeply understood.